Praise for
Beth Vrabel

"Vrabel takes three knotty, seemingly disparate
problems—bullying, the plight of wolves, and coping with
disability—and with tact and grace knits them
into an engrossing whole of despair and redemption."
—Kirkus Reviews, starred review

"Vrabel displays a canny understanding
of middle-school vulnerability."
—Booklist

"[Vrabel's] challenging subject matter is handled in a gentle,
age-appropriate way with humor and genuine affection."
—School Library Journal

"Beth Vrabel weaves an authentic, emotional journey
that makes her a standout among debut authors."
—Kerry O'Malley Cerra, author of Just a Drop of Water

"Vrabel tackles some tough issues, including albinism,
depression, and loneliness, with a compassionate perspective
and a charming voice."
*—Amanda Flower, author of
Agatha Award-nominated Andi Boggs series*

"Beth Vrabel's stellar writing captivates readers from the start
as she weaves a powerful story of friendship and hardship."
—Buffy Andrews, author of The Lion Awakens and Freaky Frank

"Beth Vrabel doesn't shy away from the tough stuff
that can complicate the lives of tweens."
—Melissa Hart, author of Avenging the Owl

THE RECKLESS CLUB

BETH VRABEL

RP|KIDS
PHILADELPHIA

Running Press Kids
Hachette Book Group
1290 Avenue of the Americas, New York, NY 10104
www.runningpress.com/rpkids
@RP_Kids

Printed in the United States of America

First Edition: October 2018

Published by Running Press Kids, an imprint of Perseus Books, LLC,
a subsidiary of Hachette Book Group, Inc. The Running Press Kids name
and logo is a trademark of the Hachette Book Group.

The Hachette Speakers Bureau provides a wide range
of authors for speaking events. To find out more, go to
www.hachettespeakersbureau.com or call (866) 376-6591.

The publisher is not responsible for websites (or their content)
that are not owned by the publisher.

Print book cover and interior design by Frances J. Soo Ping Chow

Library of Congress Control Number: 2017959764

ISBNs: 978-0-7624-9040-0 (hardcover), 978-0-7624-9039-4 (ebook)

LSC-C

10   9   8   7   6   5   4   3   2   1

FOR K.A.

Dear Student,

You know why I'm contacting you.

You decided to mar your last day of middle school with a reckless decision, one that ordinarily would land you in a day of in-school suspension. Perhaps you thought being a freshman and moving up to the high school would mean you're exempt from that punishment. You are not.

However, you are hereby offered an opportunity to begin your next year on a better foot than you ended the last. I am willing to allow you to spend the last day of summer vacation at Northbrook Retirement Village for a day of service. You will be expected to care for the needs of residents as well as spend a significant portion of the day reflecting on your poor decisions and what you have learned by helping others in need. This will be demonstrated in the form of an essay to me, due at the end of the day.

This invitation will be extended to several other students who also behaved regretfully. It is my hope that each of you will spend this time not only gaining a greater understanding of your own autonomy but also reflecting on what might have led to—and prevented—the decisions of your classmates.

Enjoy your summer,
Principal Hardy

AUGUST
23

8:00 a.m.

JASON "The Nobody"

Jason sits on the grass lawn outside the Northbrook Retirement Village, curled over the sketchbook on his lap and putting off the inevitable as long as possible. A mud-colored Volvo pulls to a stop in front of him; all of the windows are down but even if they weren't, he'd be able to hear the high-pitched squeals from inside.

"I can't believe you couldn't get me out of this!" a girl screeches. Jason doesn't bother looking up. He'd know Lilith Bhat's voice anywhere. It had always echoed through the halls of Northbrook Middle School.

"Lily, you need to be held accountable for your actions." The

4

woman in the driver's seat sounds distracted. Jason peeks up; sure enough, he can see through the window that her mom's thumbing through screens on her phone.

"Lilith. My name is *Lilith*. You gave it to me. Why can't you use it?"

Her mom sighs, and Jason hears the car shift into park. "Your father gave you that name. I wanted to give you a traditional Indian name—Bharati, another name for Saraswati, the goddess of wisdom."

"You're an atheist," Lilith snaps. Jason bends further over the sketchbook to hide his chuckle, while keeping his eyes on the car. "And, seriously? You would've named me Bharati? I'd be Bharati Bhat! That name is awful."

"It's your grandmother's name."

"Like I said. Even Dida wouldn't want that for me."

"You could use a little wisdom."

Lilith crosses her arms and slams her back against the seat.

Her mother sighs again. "Stop being so dramatic."

Lilith throws her arms in the air, then whips open the car door. "Don't be dramatic?" She leans into her mother; she's about as opposite of Lilith as a person can get, with a dark suit and her hair carefully combed back into a tight ponytail. "It's like we've never met."

Mrs. Bhat presses her thin lips into a pale line. She slowly closes her eyes. "Perhaps you could use this time to *learn* something."

Lilith pauses before stepping out of the car. "I suppose I could."

She stands outside of the car now, running her hands through her glossy black-brown hair to make sure it's smooth. She tugs at her dress—it's bright orange and snug across the top before flaring out. Some girls with Lilith's soft shape hide under big sweaters or loose T-shirts. But the bright orange is meant to draw attention, Jason knows; everything Lilith does is to get attention. The orange complements her dark skin, and the retro style of the dress makes her look more like a 1950s-era teenager than a thirteen-year-old middle schooler in middle Missouri. "I *could* use this time to study the elderly, in case I'm ever cast in a time-traveling story. They're back in vogue."

Jason hears her mother sigh again, then the Volvo is pushed into drive. "That's not what I meant. I'll pick you up at four thirty, Lily." She peels away from the curb, making the passenger side door slam shut as Lilith jumps out of the way.

"It's Lil*ith*!" she yells at the retreating car. Whipping around, she spots him. Her eyes widen like she's never seen him before, even though they had four classes together last year. Jason feels her eyes drifting across him, taking in his shaggy hair and a beanie. "What are you looking at?"

Jason shrugs and smiles with just the right side of his mouth.

His choppy, long hair hangs across his narrow eyes. He nibbles at a hangnail, and Lilith winces at his painted-black chewed-up fingernails.

"You have abysmal cuticle care."

"I'll work on that."

Lilith crosses her arms and stomps toward the door. After shoving the sketchbook and charcoal pencil into his backpack, Jason trails silently behind her. He gives her a lot of space because drama might be contagious and he doesn't want anything to do with it. He keeps his hands shoved in his pockets, his head bent low, and his posture as slouched as the canvas backpack slung over his shoulder.

"Hey, Picasso." A girl with close-cropped pixie hair and eyes heavily lined with black makeup is perched on the cement ledge bordering the building's porch.

"Rex." Jason nods hello.

Rex tilts her head toward the doors closing behind Lilith. "Is there, like, a school meeting going on? First Drama Queen—"

"I think she wants to be called Lilith."

"What? Anyway, inside I spotted the black kid with the"— Rex presses a finger into her cheek like a dimple and makes a sound—*ding*—like a crystal goblet being flicked—"with Principal Hardy, probably sweet-talking the nurses into a giving him a foot massage."

Jason's eyes crinkle. "Wes is here? He's, like, class president. I wonder what he did wrong to serve time."

"Serve time?"

"You know, suspension? I didn't mean to offend, like if serving time is something you or your fam—"

"Your political correctness is annoying." Rex crosses her arms and juts her pointy chin at Jason, who unconsciously takes a step back. "But what are you talking about?"

"Well, Principal Hardy thinks he's sticking it to us, doesn't he? Making us spend our last Saturday of summer vacation volunteering with old people since we screwed up the last day of school."

Rex squints at him.

"That's why *you're* here, right?" Jason asks.

Both turn as a red convertible screeches to a stop in front of them. Without saying good-bye or looking back at the driver, a girl in running leggings and a zipped-up sweatshirt hops out. Jason's spine seems to straighten on its own when he sees who it is—Ally. His backpack suddenly feels a lot heavier. He never would've risked bringing his sketchbook if he had known Ally was going to be here. The bag drops down his arm and he clutches it in his fist while thinking about the drawings of her midkick at the soccer net. At the finish line of the track. Pitching the softball. It's not that he's a stalker or anything, or even that he has a crush on the girl. Sports aren't his thing. Girls, either, if he's being honest. In fact, he and Ally have zilch in common.

It's just her face is made for sketching—heart-shaped but with sharp, high cheekbones incredible for shading; thick dark eyelashes framing sea-glass green eyes; even darker eyebrows in fierce straight lines like two slashes across her delicate face; wild hair that moves even more than she does. Drawing her midmovement never truly captures her, so of course he can't stop drawing her. It's an artist thing, he tells himself.

"Great." Rex groans. "Sports Barbie is here, too."

As Ally trots from the car, she shoves her thick hair back to the top of her head, not bothering to pull the hair all the way through the ponytail holder. When she gets to the stairs, she twists her neck, and Rex and Jason both cringe at the popping sound. Her father yells from the car. "Don't forget you're missing practice for this today. You better figure out a way to get in some training!"

The girl scowls, but dutifully sprints up the stairs, still without looking back.

"Ally, right?" Jason says as she passes. Rex's eyes widen. It's not like him to offer up casual conversation.

But Ally barely nods. She shoves through the door and into the building.

"*Ally, right?*" Rex mocks.

"What?" Jason ducks his head, his hair covering his eyes but not the flush across his face.

"Dude. You can't call me out on not knowing Wes's name and then say, '*Ally, right?*' as if everyone and their brother doesn't know who Sports Barbie is. She's, like, the most popular girl in school. Maybe in the county."

"I'm working on my social skills." He shrugs.

"You hate people. It's the basis of our friendship."

"We're not friends," Jason says. "I'm just the only person who isn't scared of you."

Rex's eyebrow pops up.

"Okay," he concedes, "I'm a *little* scared of you."

The corner of Rex's mouth tugs back in an almost-smile. "As you should be, Picasso." The smile disappears altogether when they hear the booming voice of their school principal ordering Ally, Wes, and Lilith to take a seat in the lobby.

"Guess we better get this over with." Rex groans. She elbows Jason in the ribs. "Maybe you can spend the day with *Ally*, working on your *social skills*."

"Shut up."

Principal Hardy is in the middle of the lobby, standing like always with his hands behind him as he gazes with narrowed eyes at Lilith, who's applying a layer of lip gloss; Ally, who's sitting on the edge of the couch with her arms crossed; and Wes, who's grinning straight back into the principal's face. Rex whistles as she saunters into the room. One of Hardy's thick gray eyebrows nudges up when he spots her. He curls a finger, indicating her to move toward him.

Rex shoves a hand through her stubby bangs, makes a fist, and tugs, then trudges toward the principal. "What's up?"

Hardy crosses his arms. "It's a positive sign that you're here."

"Wait!" says Wes, the boy with the *ding* smile. "This was optional?" He salutes the rest of the students and moves toward the door.

"Sit down! No, mister. It's not," Mr. Hardy bellows, but keeps his eyes locked with Rex. Wes sits back down.

Rex stares at the principal, but doesn't say anything. The longer the silence stretches, the deeper Hardy's face flushes as he waits for Rex to crack and be the first to speak. Instead, she yawns, wide and deliberate. Hardy's nostrils flare as if he's keeping his own yawn inside.

The principal speaks softly, probably so only Rex can hear, but of course the other students lean in to eavesdrop. "This is a day where you can show me you have a place at our school."

"Sorry, Teach," Rex says. "We're off to the high school this year. New principal."

Hardy smirks. "Actually, you're looking at the new high school principal. But that doesn't mean this isn't a chance for you to kick-off the new year with a clean slate."

Rex slowly blinks.

"I'm going to come down hard on you this year, Rex. No more of your games. I won't tolerate it, regardless of what you might be dealing with at . . . home."

Rex's eyes narrow. Her chin pops up. But she still doesn't speak. The two of them glare for another long moment, while behind them the other students stare without breathing.

"My money's on Rex," Wes whispers. Jason backs away from the other boy.

Principal Hardy grinds his teeth. "Take a seat," he finally snaps.

Rex backs up, eyes still on the principal, and sinks into the seat next to Lilith.

"You're on my dress," Lilith whines, pulling her skirt from under Rex's legs.

"Whose is it, your mom's?" Rex doesn't budge.

"This is *vintage*," Lilith says importantly. She yanks on the skirt, pulling it out from under Rex.

Rex hisses like a cat, making two bright red spots flare on Lilith's cheeks and a laugh escape from Wes. Rex turns her glare on him, but he seems impervious, smiling even wider. Rex claps silently as Lilith, her skirt yanked free, makes a big production of grabbing her satchel—also vintage, plastic with giant peonies— before stomping over to the other vinyl couch in the lobby. She

12

plops down next to Ally, who sighs out of her nose and angles away from all of them.

"Seriously," Lilith whispers to Jason too loudly to actually be a whisper. Jason's eyes widen at being directly addressed. "How can you be *friends* with her?" Ally turns their way, listening in. Jason's hands fly up like he's holding back Lilith's words.

"I'm not!" Jason stumbles to his feet. His head whips between Lilith, Rex, and Ally. Rex stretches out her legs, crossing them at the ankles, and watches Jason squirm. "I mean, Rex, you're not really friends with anyone, are you? I don't mean that, either. I mean, you don't like people. Right? It's not that I don't want to be—"

Wes takes a seat next to Rex, rubbing his hands together. "Oooh, this is getting good." He nudges her. "You're going to hurt him, aren't you?"

But Jason's off the hook as Rex turns on Wes, her lips curling back like she's about to hiss again.

"Meow," Wes whispers with another *ding* smile that only stretches when he realizes he's thrown her. Rex is first to look away.

Three loud claps from Principal Hardy and four out of the five students turn toward him. Rex stays put, staring at a fish tank instead of the principal and the squat woman in scrubs next to him.

"Oh, hi there, Rex!" the woman says suddenly. Still, Rex doesn't move. Jason's head swivels between the two of them as if looking for the connection.

The woman bounces a little at them, a smile stretching across her face.

"This is Mrs. Mitchell, head of Northbrook Retirement Village," Hardy says.

"Jeff and I go way back!" Mrs. Mitchell says with a laugh, not seeing Mr. Hardy's wince.

"Oh, yeah?" Wes says.

"That's right," Mrs. Mitchell says. She clasps her hands behind her back and rocks back on her heels. "Jeff here thinks running a middle school is *so hard*." She rolls her eyes as she drags out the last two words. "I said, 'You should try a nursing home sometime if you think you've got it rough!' And that's how we got here, I guess."

"That's one way of looking at it," Mr. Hardy says without a smile. "Mrs. Mitchell is my sister."

"And we're going to join forces today! Jeff and I have so many fun things planned for y'all!"

"You're not Southern, Trish. We were raised in Pennsylvania. You can't pull off a Southern accent. How many times do I have to tell you?"

Mrs. Mitchell's smile stays plastered on her face. "Jeff," she drawls to the kids, "might learn today how important it is to be warm and homey when prompting a change in behavior."

Mr. Hardy shakes his head. "I think I'll stick with my style."

"Which is what?" Mrs. Mitchell asks.

Wes's hand shoots in the air, but Mr. Hardy cuts him off. "Don't answer that, Wes." He clears his throat, then continues, "Mrs. Mitchell and I have worked to help coordinate today's activities."

"Activities?" Ally asks. "I thought we were helping to clean or something."

"No, no," Mrs. Mitchell says, her smile stretching even farther. "We have so many fun activities planned. *I* feel that contributing to society is what brings about change, not *isolating* people for wrongdoing. So we'll be doing fun things—crafts, preparing meals, maybe even something *artistic*—I just can't wait!" She claps like a walrus Jason once saw at a zoo.

"You're going to love it here!" Mrs. Mitchell continues. "It's so fun and so *well run* that you'll never want to leave."

Principal Hardy forces a crack-in-cement smile despite the audible groan from every student. "Mrs. Mitchell says she wouldn't miss an opportunity to have you interact socially with residents."

Jason's eyes flick between Hardy and Rex, who stood up abruptly at Mrs. Mitchell's words. Hardy shakes his head ever so slightly, eyes locked with Rex. She slumps back into the seat. No one but Jason seems to have noticed the exchange. Jason's fingers drum on his backpack as he leans against an armchair, a safe place outside of the drama on the two couches.

"Our seniors *love* to talk with young people," says Mrs. Mitchell, bouncing a little more. "First, I'll pair you each with someone who could use a great listening ear." She tugs on her ear and winks. Rex slams her head on the couch back.

"Interview them, ask questions, get to know them," Principal Hardy instructs.

Lilith runs her hands over her dress so the pleats stay smooth. "That's exactly what I was planning to do—approach this as research for future method acting."

"Acting?" Mrs. Mitchell claps her hands together. "You're an actress?"

Lilith nods and says, "I've been the lead in all the community and middle school productions."

"I thought that new kid, the blonde, was going to be the lead last time?" Wes cuts in.

"That was a last-minute casting change," Lilith says primly. *That's one way of putting it,* Jason thinks but keeps his mouth shut. "The point is," she continues, "yes. I am an actress."

"Casting change?" Ally says. "I heard you went all Hulk backstage?"

16

"Oh," says Mrs. Mitchell, saving Lilith from replying. "The residents here *love* performances!" More frantic bouncing, this time with claps. "You could put on a skit for them!"

"A what?" Ally and Rex say at the same time, then scowl at each other before turning to glare in different directions.

"A skit." The smug smile stretching across Principal Hardy's face is Grinch-like and slow. "I like the sound of that. I'm also going to need a full-page letter—front *and* back—from each of you outlining what you learned throughout the course of the day."

"Yes!" Mrs. Mitchell cheers again. "At four o'clock, we have a half hour allotted for entertainment. Generally, we play bingo or charades, but I know the residents would much prefer watching an original skit!" She squeals. "Especially if it's *inspired by their own lives!*" Clap, clap, clap. Bounce, bounce, bounce. "Oh, this is fabulous."

"Fabulous," Wes echoes, and the dimple disappears from his cheek as he shakes his head. All four turn Rex-like death glares on Lilith, who once again straightens her dress.

"Thanks a lot, Lily," Ally hisses.

"It's Lil*ith*."

"Okay," Mrs. Mitchell says, "let's meet our seniors! You can get to know them while helping to serve breakfast. If you'll leave your bags here, I'll have one of the aides put them in the meeting room where you'll be having lunch."

The kids slip their phones into their pockets and drop their bags in front of Mrs. Mitchell, all except for Jason. "I'll hang on to mine," he says.

Lilith grabs her satchel back, too.

Mrs. Mitchell claps and bounces again, then turns, making her way past the giant tank full of tropical fish and down a hallway. Principal Hardy sighs and swoops up his arms like a conductor. The students groan and follow her. That is, all except for Rex, whose eyes stay locked on the fish tank, where a fat purple fish glides backward and then rushes forward into its own reflection again and again. Jason pauses beside her.

Hardy clears his throat. Silently, Rex stands and trails behind the rest of the group toward the cafeteria.

"Don't worry," Hardy says as Rex passes. "We're staying off the third floor."

"As if I care," Rex snaps, and barrels ahead, elbowing Jason to the side.

"What's on the third floor?" Jason asks the principal.

But Principal Hardy just shakes his head. Under his breath, he says, "Don't forget why you're here, Jason."

9:00 a.m.

LILITH "The Drama Queen"

Lilith scans the cafeteria. It's a sea of gray. People with gray hair and pale skin shoveling gray lumps of oatmeal into their mouths. The residents sit around large round tables, talking to one another, or, in some cases, to their oatmeal. *Everybody has a story*, Lilith reminds herself over the thump of her heart that sounds a lot like a stopwatch. *They all just look boring. Underneath, I'm sure they're all very exciting people.*

"Okay," Mrs. Mitchell says with another bounce and clap. "Let's partner up, shall we?" Mrs. Mitchell strides up to a tiny woman with wispy white hair on an otherwise mostly bald, wrinkled head. Lilith is reminded of a dandelion gone to puff atop a narrow yellowing stem. The woman's mouth flops open and a noise like the snap of a lid on a Tupperware container leaks out.

Mrs. Mitchell glances at the clipboard in her hands. "All right, *Ally.*"

Lilith gives a quick prayer of thanks for alphabetical order as Mrs. Mitchell leans forward and wipes a little drool from the corner of the woman's mouth with a paper napkin.

"Opal, this is Ally," Mrs. Mitchell bellows. "She's going to get to know you a bit."

Ally swallows hard and takes a step back, right onto Jason's foot. He grimaces but says, "It's okay," as if she had apologized. She ignores him, her eyes flicking from side to side. She then sidesteps into Lilith, who pushes her forward.

"Is there anyone else—?" Ally murmurs, but Mrs. Mitchell is now leaning toward Opal.

"Ally is going to help you with your breakfast today, Opal." The old lady blinks wide blue eyes. Her mouth stretches into a toothless smile. "Oh, you forgot your teeth again today, didn't you?" Mrs. Mitchell laughs and pulls out a chair for Ally.

Ally doesn't budge.

"Go ahead," says Mrs. Mitchell, pointing to the chair.

Ally stares at Opal and then down at the tray in front of the old woman, filled with small containers of applesauce and oatmeal.

She glances at Opal's curled, bony hands resting on her thin lap. Ally grips her stomach with one hand and takes another step back, shaking her head. This time Jason moves with her. "I'll take Opal," he whispers, and smiles at the old woman.

But Opal reaches out and grabs Ally's hand. She tries to slip her hand out of the old woman's knotty grasp while her eyes dart around the loud, bright cafeteria. Jason places his hand on her shoulder. Ally shudders, but finally sits in the plastic seat in front of Opal.

"That's it," Mrs. Mitchell says. "Just give her a few spoonfuls of food, okay?"

Jason takes the seat next to Ally without waiting for Mrs. Mitchell's introduction. Across from him a man who looks to be in his nineties smiles and blinks his cloudy eyes.

"I'm Mike," he says to Jason.

Great, Lilith thinks, *no way could my person be worse than theirs.*

Mrs. Mitchell nods and writes *Mike* next to Jason's name. The old man nods. Jason nods. Both turn toward Opal and Ally.

"Come along, children." Mrs. Mitchell beckons Wes, Rex, and Lilith toward the opposite end of the cafeteria. She stands in front of a frail-looking woman smiling blandly up at them. Her gray hair is in a knot at the back of her head. She's knitting something with blue and orange yarn.

Wes and Rex take a tandem step backward just as Mrs. Mitchell turns, leaving Lilith front and center.

"Perfect! Lilith!" Mrs. Mitchell says. "Now, Agnes, this is Lilith. She's going to ask you questions so she can write a skit about you!"

"About me?" Agnes chuckles. "Why, it's going to be the most boring skit ever. I've called this little town home my whole life. All ninety-two years of it!"

"Oh," says Lilith, "I'm sure you've done *something* interesting in nine decades."

Agnes's bottom lip pops out as she considers. "I made a quilt once."

Lilith leans over to Mrs. Mitchell. "Are you sure there isn't anyone else who might be a better fit for *me*?"

But Mrs. Mitchell just pulls out the chair and moves to another table, with Rex and Wes trailing behind.

"Now, I've saved the best for last. You two are in for a treat. Hubert and Grace have the most wonderful stories to share! They grew up together, but just got married two years ago—right here at Northbrook!"

"Hold up!" Lilith rushes forward and grabs Rex's arm. She quickly drops it under Rex's death glare and grabs Wes's instead. Rex slumps into the seat in front of the old man.

Lilith hisses at Wes, "This is my old lady. You can have Agnes."

Wes glances at Agnes, who's clicking her knitting needles and humming, and then looks back at Grace, who's adding another electric blue layer of nail polish to her fingernails, laughing raucously at something Hubert just whispered in her ear. His eyes slide to Rex, slouched across from the lovebirds. "Not a chance."

"Oh, Lilith!" Agnes calls out. "They're passing out oatmeal! I just love oatmeal. Oatmeal, oatmeal, oatmeal!"

Lilith scrunches shut her eyes and shudders. "I'm going to the bathroom first," she calls out to Agnes. Under her breath, she adds, "To pray to Saraswati for wisdom on how to make a skit out of the world's lamest old lady."

As Lilith stomps away, Agnes says down to her knitting needles, "I lived on dry oatmeal for those three days I spent drifting in the middle of the Atlantic on a piece of plywood. Just me and Quaker Oats. Soaked the rest in the saltwater to make little balls"—she mimes rolling dough with her knotty hands—"that I'd throw at the sharks if they got too close."

"What's that, dear?" Mrs. Mitchell calls out as she waters the plants around the room.

"Oh, just how much I love oatmeal," Agnes replies. "Oatmeal, oatmeal, oatmeal!"

Mrs. Mitchell smiles. "Sweet, simple Agnes."

9:15 a.m.

WES "The Flirt"

Short of wearing a sandwich box sign that read BACK OFF, Rex gives off every indication she is not interested in getting to know anyone, most of all Wes. All of which makes her even more interesting to everyone.

Clearly Rex just doesn't know him well enough yet. Wes sinks into the seat next to her, letting his legs spill out and arms fall at his sides. Rex narrows her eyes at the spot where his leg is barely an inch from hers. Slowly, he shifts his a little farther away.

"So, what did you two do to be sentenced to a day of shoveling creamed carrots into our old pie holes?" Grace asks. She waves her just-painted fingers in the air until Hubert nabs her hands and gently blows on them.

"Uh . . ." Wes's ever-present smile slips a little at Grace's question. He shakes his head to dislodge the memory of cruel laughter and his favorite teacher's face crumpling. "It was a big misunderstanding."

Rex snorts.

"What?" Maybe that's why she acts like she hates him. Maybe she knows the truth about that day.

"Everyone always says it's a misunderstanding," Rex says in a bored voice. "Whatever you did, own it."

"What'd *you* do?" Wes asks.

"Nothing." Rex crosses her arms.

This time, Wes snorts.

"Whatever."

"You had to do something. No one would be here if not." Wes glances at Grace, *ding* smile back in place. "No offense."

"None taken, dearie," she says, giggling as Hubert kisses her fingertips.

Rex shudders.

Wes nudges her again. "Does the sight of true love bother you?"

"Of course not. There's no such thing as true love."

All three of them—Wes, Grace, and Hubert—stare at Rex with mouths agape.

Wes shakes his head. "You don't believe in true love? Everyone believes in true love."

"It's what woke Snow White," Grace adds.

"It's what brought us together," says Hubert, holding up Grace's hand in his own. "It took us sixty-five years and the passing of both of our first spouses"—both he and Grace cross their hearts with their unclenched hands—"but true love brought us here."

"Yes," Grace says. "We spotted each other across the bingo room, and it was like being in high school all over again. Only this time, I asked him out right away."

"Asked him out?" Wes cut in. "Where do you go out when you live here?"

"Oh, you know," Hubert says, "to the porch."

"And the *swing*," Grace says in a singsongy voice.

Suddenly the two of them are cheek to cheek, swaying gently back and forth, back and forth, singing softly. "And we were a-swinging . . . a swinging. . . ."

Rex covers her eyes with her fists. When she looks up again, the old couple is still singing. Grumbling, she jumps to her feet and stomps toward the water fountain in the corner of the room.

When she turns around, of course Wes is right there, leaning against the wall. "What's your problem with love?"

"Nothing. How could I have a problem with something that

doesn't exist?" Rex pushes by Wes, knocking his back against the wall.

He grabs her elbow to stop her. Quickly she whips around, jerking her elbow out of his hand and shoving him against the wall, intentionally this time.

"Don't touch me!" she hisses, her face fierce and eyes wild. "Don't you *ever* touch me!"

"Sorry! Sorry!" Wes holds up his hands. "I won't touch you again. I swear!"

Rex shoves him again, knocking his shoulder blades against the cinder block, then backs away.

"What's wrong with you?" Wes whispers as she stomps off. She grabs the chair she had been sitting in and drags it to the edge of the cafeteria table, facing toward the hall and away from Grace and Hubert.

Wes huffs out a deep breath and shakes his head but can't lose the image of Rex's face inches from his. She wasn't just angry. She had looked panicked. Jason, the quiet kid, is watching him from behind his fringe of hair. Wes smirks and shrugs in a *can-you-believe-that-girl?* way. Jason doesn't smile—just turns toward the old lady Ally is trying to feed. Ally's hands are shaking so badly that the applesauce splashes from the spoon across the old lady's cheek. Jason, Wes notices, is sitting on his hands.

Wes glances around to see if anyone else saw Rex's freak-out.

27

Lilith, her face red and nostrils flaring, is sitting across from a woman singing about oatmeal balls. Principal Hardy has his back to the room, yelling something into a cell phone, and Mrs. Mitchell is clapping for two men playing ping-pong in the far corner of the room. Wes's eyes settle on Rex, or, more precisely, on the back of her head. Her short hair is a few different lengths, like she grabbed hunks of it and hacked at it with a pair of scissors. He realizes this is probably exactly what she had done and felt another surge of . . . something. Curiosity, maybe?

He moves back to the table. Hubert and Grace are snuggling and singing, and, for some reason, the sound now grates on Wes's ears. He sits on a different chair; it's close to Rex but still far enough away.

Rex is shooting death beams at a nurse in pink-and-blue teddy bear scrubs.

Finally, Wes stands and drags his seat next to hers.

"Are you freaking kidding me?" Rex groans.

"What's your problem with Teddy Bear Nurse over there?" When Rex turns toward him, Wes holds up his hands in a pose of surrender. He breathes out as she slumps back in her seat.

"I hate her." Rex tilts away from Wes toward the nurse.

"Why?"

"Why do you care?"

"I'm interested."

"Don't be."

"Can't help it," Wes says.

"I don't like you," Rex replies.

"That's okay. I like you." And it's not until he says it that Wes feels it for real. He *does* like her, even though she doesn't like him back. Maybe it's *because* she doesn't like him back. Everyone likes him and so they aren't as likable to him.

Rex whips around to him, two red splotches on her cheeks, and Wes realizes he's startled the unshakeable Rex Gallagher.

Wes grins. *Ding!*

"You better not be messing with me."

"I'm not. You're interesting."

Rex sighs as Teddy Bear Nurse disappears behind the kitchen's swinging door. "It's going to be a long day."

"Plenty of time to get to know each other." *Ding!*

"Stop doing that."

"Doing what?"

"Smiling."

Before he can answer, Mrs. Mitchell claps her hands and calls out, "Do any of you children need to use the little boys' or little girls' rooms?"

All five hands shoot into the air.

"All right," she sing-songs as she leads them toward the exit. "Principal Hardy has had to leave for a spell." Her voice lowers.

"From what I gathered, two teachers started fighting over who gets Smart Boards in their classrooms and so he needs to mediate the argument over at the school." Her mouth twitches as she delivers the news. She bounces a little and claps again. "So, let's just go to the restrooms, and then we can work on those skits!"

A crash and subsequent yelling makes all of them whip around toward the ping-pong table. One of the players has his paddle up in the air like a sword, swinging it toward the other player, who takes aim and throws the white ball at the first player's forehead.

"Miserable cheat!" the ball-thrower bellows.

"Aargh! No one calls me a cheat!" The other player launches after the first, who ducks behind the table.

"Oh dear," Mrs. Mitchell says, and heads toward the old men. "Can you all follow the signs on the wall? The bathrooms are at the end of the next hallway. Let's meet back here in, oh, ten minutes or so? I've got to deal with this."

"Let's go," Lilith says, and strides out the door. "Agnes is making her way over here to bore me to death."

Wes and Jason wince in unison as the paddle-hoisting ping-pong player kicks at the hiding ball-throwing player. The man drops the paddle and wobbles on one leg.

"Ha!" the hiding player taunts. "Kicked my artificial knee. Titanium! Hope you get a hematoma, you cheat!"

Agnes, now beside them, shakes her head. "They're terrible

fighters. When I got my first black belt, I fought three master belts at once. And not once did I kick anyone in the knee."

"Your first black belt?" Wes asks.

Agnes bows. "One in tae kwon do, one in kung fu, and a third in judo. But kickboxing is my favorite. Favorite, favorite, favorite."

Lilith pops her head back in the door. "Are you guys coming or not? Ally is running up and down stairs for some stupid reason, and Rex took off. She's bailing on writing this skit, I just know it."

"Where's Ally?" Jason asks.

"At the stairs, but—"

"Thanks, see ya!" Jason darts past Lilith and Wes.

Agnes sings, "Favorite, favorite, favorite!" She exits through the door, as well, waving good-bye to Lilith.

Rolling her eyes, Lilith says, "Yes, Agnes, I know. Oatmeal's your favorite." To Wes, she says, "So, are you coming?"

But Wes has been scanning the cafeteria, looking for the nurse in teddy bear scrubs. "Which way did Rex go?"

Lilith points down the hall, and Wes takes off, ignoring Lilith's, "What about the *skit*?"

Trotting down the hall, Wes finally spots Rex. She's trailing Teddy Bear Nurse, who's too focused on the iPad in her hands to notice, just like Rex is too focused on her to notice Wes. All of the nurses seem to use iPads instead of paper files, and Teddy Bear Nurse thumbs through the screen, her eyes on it instead of where she's going. When she bumps into a wheelchair outside a patient's room, Rex leans against the wall, cramming her hand against her mouth to keep from laughing. Wes grins and picks up his steps. The nurse glances at the doorway of the resident's room, peers inside, and then continues down the hall. Rex ducks her head and turns her back on the nurse but doesn't catch Wes trailing her. When Rex turns again, the nurse is striding into a room. Rex pauses to stare at the door—each patient has a printer paper–sized photograph of him- or herself taped to the door. Even from where he stands, Wes can make out the face. It's the woman with fluffy white hair that Ally had been paired with in the cafeteria.

"Figures," Rex mutters. "Someone too weak to defend herself." She curls her hands into fists at her side.

Just as she begins to dart forward, Wes trots toward her. "Hey!"

Rex throws up her arms. She grabs his arm and yanks him into an open room as Teddy Bear Nurse glances back.

"You almost wrecked the whole thing!" Rex whisper-screams at Wes.

He knocks into a tray table, toppling the framed photos on top. "What whole thing?" he asks, picking up one of the displaced photos.

"Yes!" says a shaky voice from the corner. "What whole thing?"

Both kids jump and turn toward the person speaking. It's Agnes, the senior Lilith had been paired with in the cafeteria. Wes's jaw drops a little as he looks around the tiny room, which is dim, lit only by lamps covered in brightly colored scarves. The window frame, tray table behind him, and shelves are jammed full of stuff—trophies, laminated newspaper clippings, photo albums, dried flowers, a small blue glass bottle, and dozens of framed photographs. Most of the photographs show Agnes as a young woman. He glances at the one in his hand; it's a teenage Agnes with her hair in long thick braids, and she's standing on an elephant, her arms outstretched like a T.

"Just behind you, dear," Agnes says. "Just put that with the others behind you. Those are from my circus days."

Wes rights the photo on the tray as Rex peeks out the door.

"Is that—" He shakes his head, squints, and looks again. The bookshelf behind him is piled with knickknacks and collectibles. The dim light glints against a golden statuette of a man with clasped hands. Wes tilts his head, staring at the statue. "Is that—" he starts again.

"Oh!" says Agnes, clapping her hands. "My Hollywood days!" She waves her arms through the air as if dancing a hula and begins to hum.

Again Wes shakes his head. "But didn't you say you never lived anywhere but here?"

Still dancing—now shaking her hips, too—Agnes smiles. "Well, no other place has ever been *home*."

"But—"

Rex grabs Wes's wrist and yanks him toward the door. "She's getting away. We have to go."

"Who's getting away?" Wes twists out of her grip.

Agnes, still dancing the hula, answers, "She's following that awful nurse, that's who."

Rex's eyes turn to marbles. "You know her? I mean, you know that she's awful?"

"The worst," Agnes sing-songs. "Worst, worst, worst."

"What did she do to *you*?" Rex asks.

"Oh, nothing, dear," Agnes replies. "I'd axe kick her if she got too close. You think she's got sticky fingers, don't you? Can't say she does. Can say she's mean as the dickens, though. Never lets us have any fun." Agnes twists in a circle, still dancing. Wes notices that she's wearing slippers with giant owl heads over the toes.

"Well, I'm going to prove she steals stuff," Rex announces.

"Did you *see* her take something?" Wes asks.

"Not today." Rex crosses her arms.

Wes rocks back on his heels. "Wow, you must've done something huge for Hardy to sentence you to multiple days of service."

Rex glares at him and doesn't answer.

"Fine, fine. Keep your secrets." Wes crosses his arms, too,

mimicking her pose. "For now, anyway."

"Go on back to the others. I've got this."

Wes grins.

"*Ding*," Rex mutters, which only serves to widen Wes's smile.

"Nah," he says, "*we've* got this."

"Not necessary," Rex snaps. She peeks out the door again. "You're just going to slow me down."

"How long have you been trying to catch her in the act?" Wes asks.

Without thinking, Rex answers, "Six months."

Wes blinks at her a moment. *Did Hardy make her volunteer for six months? What had she done? What was she hiding?* He swallows the questions, knowing Rex will never answer. Instead, he focuses on the only thing she seems willing to open up about—Teddy Bear Nurse. "You haven't caught her nabbing anything in six months, and you suspect she's onto you?" Wes crosses his arms. "She's not onto me. Or Jason. Or Lilith. Or Ally."

"So what?"

"So what?" Wes half laughs. "So, you need us to help you catch her in the act."

JASON "The Nobody"

Lilith's sigh drifts past Jason as he turns the corner toward the stairwell and Ally. He passes Mike at the elevators. The old man nods at him, coughing into a big white hankie.

"Have you seen—" Jason starts, but Mike cuts him off by pointing farther down the hall.

"She's that way," the old man wheezes.

Jason thanks him just as the doors to the elevator open. "Aren't you getting on?" he asks Mike.

"I'll wait for the next one." Mike pushes his folded-up hankie into his back pocket. The elevator doors close and, once it begins moving to the next floor, Mike presses for it again.

"Are you waiting for Opal?" Jason guesses.

He just smiles. "She'll be headed this way soon. Takes her a bit to get moving sometimes."

Jason opens his mouth to say something—he doesn't know what—but then he hears the quick smack of Ally's sneakers on the stairs. Mike, coughing again, waves him away.

Jason trots down the hall, pushing his backpack up his shoulder. *Slap, slap, slap.* Ally's sneakers hit the stairs in quick succession as she sprints up them. Jason squints, seeing just a flash of her purple sneakers two flights over his head. He lets the backpack slide down his arm onto the tiled floor and slumps next to it. Unzipping the bag, he grabs his sketchbook and flips to a fresh page. He pulls the pencil from behind his ear and breathes out as his hand takes over.

The scratch of his pencil against the thick creamy paper is the only soundtrack to the steady beat of Ally's footsteps up and down the stairs. Jason's bangs fall over his forehead as he leans forward, the pencil making swoops and shades. There's a moment in drawing where his mind and his hand disconnect, where he can finally stop *thinking* before acting and just do. Just draw. His hand seems now to move on its own, the images pouring through the pencil onto the page. As easy as breathing.

If only speaking could be as simple. But Jason's thoughts clog before they reach his lips. When he does speak, he seems to say the wrong words, to just blurt out the tip-of-his-iceberg thoughts. But when he draws, everything he's feeling, everything he's sorting out, just flows.

Jason bends over the sketch as a face emerges on the page. He pauses a half second to recognize it. He had thought he was sketching Ally, but Opal emerges instead. The figure is slightly altered from reality, with Ally's darker eyebrow slashes over Opal's cloudy eyes. Opal's frizzy hair frames Ally's straight-line mouth. The two couldn't be more different in real life; how or why he was merging them didn't make any sense. But Jason doesn't pause to think about his reasons. He leans over the page, watching as if it were a movie, as his own ideas take shape. He's so lost in his creation that he misses the sudden silence of Ally's backbeat steps.

"What are you doing?" Ally's sitting on the stair just behind him, peering down at the drawing.

"Nothing." Jason whips shut the notebook, but Ally is faster. She nabs it from his hands and flips it back open to the page he had been drawing. "Is this . . . ?"

"Yeah. It's Opal." Jason pushes his hair back, painting a charcoal pencil smudge across his forehead. "It's not a big deal."

Ally sinks back onto the stair, staring at the page. Her eyes are wide. Her leg drums up and down. As Ally scans the page, Jason closes his eyes and feels his face burning.

"This is amazing," she says, and his eyes pop open. "Did you just do it?"

Jason shrugs. Again he grabs for the notebook, but Ally swerves to the side, clutching it in both hands. She shudders, then hands it back.

"What?" Jason asks. "I mean, it's just a sketch. It's not, like, ready for public consumption or anything." Not that anything he does is ever meant to be public. *Except for those two times,* he thinks, *and look how that turned out.*

"Dude, it's not the drawing that's giving me shivers. The drawing is, well, it's incredible," she says.

Jason clamps down on his tongue, trapping it in his cheek to keep from smiling.

Ally glances at him, her hazel eyes locking with his. "It's just, it's so *her*. It's like she's right in front of me."

"Opal?" Jason glances at the drawing. Opal's face is as wrinkled as if someone had crinkled up the paper and tried to smooth it out. But the corner of her eyes tilt to prep for a smile.

"I mean"—Ally shudders again—"I can see her in front of me, her mouth open for more applesauce."

Jason scratches at the back of his neck, as if coaxing the words to his throat. "She seems to like you. Seems to like you helping her, I mean."

Ally's leg drums against the step. *She never stops r*

Jason thinks. An invisible energy vibrates through Ally at all times. He thinks about how fully he falls into drawing, where the pencil against the paper is the only sound, the only action, the only thought. Did Ally have anything like that? Or was she always moving in different directions? Her leg still popping up and down, she gathers her hair into a tighter ponytail on top of her head.

"Opal," Jason starts, "she's not so bad. I think—I think maybe she's trying to tell you something."

"What could she want to tell me?" Ally's eyes narrow.

Words clog in Jason's throat, but before he can cough any up, Ally's back on her feet, ready to sprint the stairs again.

"What are you doing?" he manages to croak out.

Ally raises an eyebrow. "Getting my steps in," she says in an *isn't-it-obvious* voice.

"Why?"

Ally glances down at her wrist. She taps her watch, then twists her arm to show Jason. "I'm at sixteen thousand steps. My goal is twenty. If I squeeze in a few flights, this day won't affect my training much."

"Isn't it, like, a good thing to get ten thousand steps?"

Ally shoots a grin his way. "Yep. That's why I double it." She pushes past him.

"It's one day," Jason calls up the staircase after her. "Does it really matter if you skip it?"

"Every day counts," her voice drifts toward him.

"We're supposed to stick together," he says toward her quickly retreating back. "Mr. Hardy's going to know if we separate." *Why'd I say that? It's not even true.* Jason gently bangs the back of his head against the wall. While it isn't technically true that he and Ally were supposed to stick together, he knew Mr. Hardy wouldn't be cool with all of them scattered around the nursing home when they were supposed to be on a bathroom break.

"One more flight!" Ally huffs as she heads back down.

He crosses his arms and legs as he waits. For a moment, his eyes snag on a sign detailing the different levels of the building. First floor is for residents, meeting rooms, and the cafeteria. Second floor is for intensive care. Third is for hospice and long-term medical care. Fourth is for evaluations and rehabilitation.

As Ally reaches the end of the stairway, Wes turns around the corner. When he sees them, he throws up his hands. "Hey! Where've you guys been?"

Jason shrugs. Ally checks her watch again. She grins at the number reflecting on her wrist. Looking up, she asks, "Is Hardy back and looking for us already?"

"No, but what are you guys doing?" Wes's eyes slide back and forth between the pair. The longer he looks, the more bored Ally seems and the hotter Jason's cheeks burn. Wes's mouth tucks back in a half grin, flashing his dimple. "Huh," he says.

"What?" If Jason had been drawing his own face, flames would've burst from his cheekbones at Wes's appraising look.

Ally crosses her arms. "What's up? You looked like you are in a hurry."

The smile drops from Wes's face. He nods, suddenly serious. "I am. We need your help."

"Who's *we*?" Ally asks.

"Me and Rex."

"With what?" Jason grabs his backpack, shoving his notebook inside.

"Follow me." Wes turns the corner. Ally glances at Jason, one eyebrow cocked. He shrugs and gestures toward Wes and, for just a second, Ally smiles.

LILITH "The Drama Queen"

Lilith checks under the doors of the bathroom stalls. No feet. She stands in front of the mirror and uses the palm of her hand to smooth her hair. She swivels her head back and forth and notices the light isn't shimmering against her thick, dark hair. Sighing, she rummages in her satchel and pulls out a tiny spray bottle of coconut oil.

Even though her interest lies in Hollywood, Lilith loves Bollywood. *Never underestimate the power of cross-promotion.* Her mother never shows any interest in anything on a screen other than her laptop or phone, so Lilith asked her grandmother how the Bollywood stars keep their hair so shiny. Dida said they oil their hair and showed her how to massage a thin layer of melted coconut oil through the strands and then braid them so the follicles marinate until morning. Mom rolls her eyes whenever Lilith does it and warns her people are going to make fun of how it makes her hair smell. But Mom's so out of it, she doesn't even know how *in* coconut everything is now. Lilith ran out of the good stuff—virgin coconut oil—on Thursday and her mom *still* hasn't stopped by the store for more. She'd been settling for the cheap spray since then, but soon her hair would look like her mother's—coarse and dry. *Not that Mom cares.* All Lilith's mom cares about is the latest social injustice inflicted in the world. She's a lawyer for the ACLU and can spout off for hours on end about immigration disputes and constitutional law. *B-o-r-i-n-g*, Lilith thinks with another sigh. Her dad is just as bad—a history professor at the local university. He focuses on comparative Euro-Asian empires, whatever that means. Everything about her parents is boring.

Boring is the worst trait in the world. Nothing could be worse than being boring.

Lilith's mom doesn't even wear makeup and, therefore, neither can Lilith. She digs deeper in her satchel to the diary at the bottom. Spinning the little combo lock, she clicks it open and flips the page. Lilith plucks a ruby-colored lip gloss from the hollowed-out middle of the "book" and smears it across her lips. She squeezes a dollop onto her fingertips and rubs it into her cheeks.

"Okay, Lilith," she says to her reflection, "we can do this. We can get through this day."

She closes her eyes and opens them again. "Act One, Scene One. The beautiful and wrongly convicted Lilith enters the Northbrook Retirement Village. She is a stunning starburst in an otherwise dull room. She bravely takes her seat next to the degenerate students also forced to spend their day serving the elderly."

Lilith's eyes widen, and she gently blinks before continuing her stage direction. "Tasked with creating a skit out of the punishment unfairly bestowed upon her, Lilith knows she cannot rely on the others to help. One, Rex, is a criminal. Another is Jason, a boy with too much hair hanging in his face and who might not be able to speak in full sentences. A third, Ally, is too busy showing off her muscles to care about something as important as the theater. And while the fourth, Wes, *does* have a certain charm about him, there can only be one star of this show." Lilith fluffs her now shiny hair and shoots a gleaming smile into the mirror.

Tilting her head, she says in a higher voice, "How can we aid the elderly today?"

Wiping the smile from her face, Lilith continues with the stage narration. "The students are paired with elderly patients. Lilith listens attentively while Agnes, the knitting old lady she is partnered with, babbles on and on about oatmeal." Again, Lilith adopts a wide-eyed, smiling face as she shifts into character.

"Oh, I just know you love oatmeal!" Lilith's face fills in with red. Her smile wobbles at the edges. Her wide eyes almost bulge. Finally, she lets out a guttural yell. "Even Meryl wouldn't be able to do anything with this material!"

"Lily?" someone—Ally by the sounds of it—shouts through the door. "Are you in there?"

For a moment, Lilith considers not answering. Then she shrugs. *Maybe something interesting is happening out there.*

She marches over to the door, flings it open, and stops it from swinging shut with her heel. Ally stands in front of her with the hair around her forehead a little sweat splattered, as if she just finished working out. Lilith would never allow someone to see her sweat. Lilith crosses her arms. "Have you decided to actually do your part and *help* write the skit?"

"The what?" Ally pushes past Lilith and into one of the stalls. Lilith lets the door shut as Ally squats on one of the toilets.

"Do you *mind*?" Lilith gasps. Ally is peeing without even closing the door to the stall.

"Oh, sorry. Whatever." Ally tips the stall door closed with her fingertips. "I had to go."

"Yes, but I'm right here!"

"Spend some time in a locker room. You'd get over privacy issues real quick," Ally says as she flushes. She brushes by Lilith to scrub at her hands. Instead of drying them with a paper towel, she

46

pushes them back through her hair.

Again Lilith shudders. "No, thank you." A little coconut oil would go a long way in Ally's sun-bleached, underconditioned hair.

"Listen," Ally says, "Wes needs our help."

"And I care *because* . . . ?"

Ally shakes out the remaining stray flecks of water from her fingers. "Fine, stay here, talking to yourself in the mirror."

"You heard that?" Lilith screeches.

"Duh." Ally turns to the mirror. She flexes her biceps. "Just checking out my muscles . . ."

"It was stage direction," Lilith stammers. "I didn't—"

"Whatever." Ally laughs. "I honestly do not care what *you* think of *me*. Like, even a little."

Lilith straightens. Her mouth sets into a hard line. "Great."

"Great," Ally echoes. "Let's go."

Ally stands at the door, holding it open for Lilith. For a second, Lilith hesitates. Then she sighs.

"Fine. But only because we're desperate for material."

10:01 a.m.

WES "The Flirt"

Finally Ally, with Lilith sulking behind her, comes down the hall to the lobby where the day had begun.

"Awesome," Wes says. "We're all here."

Rex leans against the wall, arms crossed and scowl fixed. "This is such a bad idea."

Wes ignores her. "Here's the deal. Teddy Bear Nurse is bad news."

"Teddy Bear Nurse?" Lilith asks.

"The nurse wearing teddy bear scrubs," Jason translates.

"What's wrong with her?" Ally pulls a hacky sack from her pocket and drops it down onto the top of her foot, dribbling it up and down, then kicking it in a perfect arch to her other foot.

"She's an evil, thieving—" Rex grumbles.

"She steals stuff," Wes interrupts. "Important stuff. From patients."

"So let's tell Hardy," Jason says. "Or that manager, Mrs. Mitchell."

"Won't work," Rex says. "Hardy doesn't care about anything going on here; he's only here to make our lives miserable and prove to his sister that he's better at taking care of us than she is at taking care of residents. And Mrs. Mitchell? I've told her, at least a dozen times. She says we don't have any proof—that Teddy Bear Nurse is the most reliable worker they have. And none of the residents have reported anything as missing."

"Wait." Ally puts up her hand. "What do you mean you told her a dozen times? I mean, I thought this was the only day we had to volunteer."

Wes clears his throat. "Rex has been here before today, okay? That's not important right now. What's important is that we have a chance to make a difference. We can be the ones who prove TBN is no good."

"Spare us the campaign-rally speech, Mr. Class President." Ally catches the hacky sack and shoves it into her back pocket.

"Look," Rex says, "if you don't want to help, don't. We'll do it without you."

"We?" Wes winks at Rex, who rolls her eyes.

"Well, what makes you think she's stealing stuff?" Lilith asks.

Jason arches an eyebrow at her then squints.

"What?" Lilith asks, catching his glance.

Jason brushes his knuckles across his cheek. "You have something, just . . . there."

Lilith's hand flies to her cheek and into a glob of red lip gloss. Lilith quickly swipes at the glob, turning it into a much more noticeable ruby-red smear across her cheek, and turns away from Jason.

"We know she's stealing stuff because Rex says she is," Wes announces, again in his *class-president leaving-no-room-for-questions* voice. "So we need to catch TBN in the act."

"How are we supposed to do that?" Lilith's voice is a long whine.

Wes pauses for a second, eyes snagging on the red streak across Lilith's face. Lilith's lips bend in a knowing smile, and he quickly looks away.

Rex rakes her hand through her hair, then digs out a tissue from her pocket. She thrusts it at Lilith and, with the other hand, motions across her cheek. "You've got junk on your face."

Lilith's mouth pops open and her face flares bright red as she grabs the tissue. She scrubs at her cheek.

"What?" Rex snorts. "Thought he was distracted by your

50

beauty, Drama Queen?"

Lilith's blush deepens as Rex laughs.

"Leave her alone," Ally says.

Rex smirks, but gestures to Wes. "Keep going, Ding."

Lilith whispers thanks to Ally, whose mouth screws up in response before turning back to Wes.

"Ding?" Wes says. She sticks her pointer in her cheek and twists. Wes grins, flashing the dimple. To the rest of them, he says, "Listen, we've got to team up. If TBN thinks we're on to her, we're not going to catch her."

"Catch her doing what?" Ally asks.

"Stealing stuff from patients." Rex, who had resumed leaning against the wall, stands upright. Wes notices a shift in how Rex is carrying herself suddenly, like she is shaken out of her usual armor. Only instead of holding her upright and tense, that armor is what keeps her constantly looking bored and, well, scary. This Rex, standing now with eyes darting to each of them, is new. She rakes a hand through her short, choppy hair, as if deciding what to say next. In a softer voice, she adds, "She goes for the ones who are too out there or too weak to stop her. She takes little stuff that they might not even miss for a long time."

"Like what?" Jason looks up from his shoes.

"Jewelry." Rex rubs at a spot just under her neck. "I know she takes jewelry. I'm not sure what else. Stuff that she can slip into her pocket."

"What are *we* supposed to do if we catch her?" Lilith twirls her bracelet around her wrist.

"Use your phone to take a photo of her in the act, if you can," Wes says.

"And follow her." Rex leans toward them a little. "She puts the stuff somewhere, a locker maybe? I've seen her tuck things in her pocket—even called her out on it to Mrs. Mitchell—but when Mitchell told her to turn out her pockets, they were empty. So I think she hides it somewhere as soon as possible so she's not caught with it."

"So we catch her and then go to Mrs. Mitchell with the evidence?" Ally bounces like she can't wait to get going.

"No!" Rex cuts in as Wes says yes. Wes steps away from the intensity of Rex's glare. "No, we have to figure out where she's putting the stuff. She'll just get rid of the evidence and I'll never—"

"You'll never what?" Jason asks.

Again Rex rubs at the spot under her neck. She shudders. "Nothing."

"I still don't understand," Lilith says, crossing her arms. "How do you know this nurse?"

Rex crosses her arms and leans back against the wall. "Think this is my first time serving detention for Hardy?"

Armor back on, Wes notes.

"But isn't this the first time he's sent people *here* for detention?" Ally asks. "I mean, I thought this was a summer break thing. Like, an experiment. That's what he told my dad, anyway."

Rex snorts. "Is it so hard to believe that Mr. Hardy would lie?" She sighs, her chest rising and falling. Rex twists her neck, making popping sounds that make Wes wince and prompt Ally to twist her own neck. Rex glances down the hall, not making eye contact with any of them. "Look, if you don't want to help, don't. I don't need you."

Wes moves closer, tilting his head so Rex is forced to look at him. "We want to help." To the rest of them, he says, "Right?"

"Right," Jason says.

Ally shrugs. "It's not like we have anything better to do."

"Except *write an entire play*!" Lilith whines.

"Fine, so Lily's out," Wes says. He shakes his head at Lilith. "Go back and sit in the cafeteria like a good little girl."

Her nostrils flaring and teeth clenched, Lilith grumbles, "I didn't say I wouldn't do it." She tosses her hair behind her shoulder. "But if I'm doing this, you *all* have to help me with the skit. And if you think I'm going to be the one to write the letter about all the things we've learned, you're *so* wrong."

Wes smiles and nods. "Sounds fair. Right?" He glances around at the rest of the group.

Ally and Jason nod.

"Whatever," Rex grumbles.

"Great," Wes says. "So here's the plan."

10:04 a.m.

LILITH "The Drama Queen"

"This plan sucks." Lilith slumps on the vinyl couch and crosses her arms and legs.

"It's not that bad," Jason says.

"*You're* not the one being used as bait." Lilith huffs.

"Stop pouting," Rex says. "You're not bait; your bracelet is."

"This bracelet is vintage." Lilith holds up her wrist, twisting it so everyone can see the thick gold bangle. Well, she is telling them it is gold, anyway. Who knows what it really is? She picked it up at the same flea market where she got her handbag. Her mom called it a waste of money and pointed out that Lilith had a half dozen real gold bracelets she never wore, even as she put yet another dusty copy of *To Kill a Mockingbird* on the counter. Her dida had given Lilith her first gold bracelet the day she was born, but she keeps that and the rest of her real jewelry tucked away in a box on her dresser and only ever wears the fake stuff. That way, it doesn't hurt at all if it breaks or no one compliments her on wearing it.

Squeaky footsteps from the hall clue them in that they're about to be interrupted. Wes straightens in the chair, plastering a wide, open smile on his face. Ally sits next to Lilith. Jason glances at the cushion next to Ally, but sits in the chair opposite Wes. Rex doesn't move.

"There you are!" Mrs. Mitchell bursts into the room and throws up her hands. "I've been looking all over this blasted place for the five of you!"

Lilith blinks. "Where else would we be?"

Mrs. Mitchell bounces on her heels. "I just told y'all to go to the restrooms! Why wouldn't you come back to the cafeteria?"

Again Lilith answers for the group. "You seemed to have your hands full in there. We thought it'd be best to stay out of the way, here, and wait for Mr. Hardy to come back."

Mrs. Mitchell puts up her hands like stop signs and waves them back and forth. "No, no, no. No need to involve Jeff in this. I'm perfectly capable of managing you while he deals with that bigger issue over at the school." She lets out her breath in a big swoop. "Well, it's good to know you're all sticking together. We're really building a community already!"

Lilith smiles and nods. "It is so inspirational, seeing the way the senior citizens band together. I suppose it inspired us, too."

Mrs. Mitchell claps and bounces. Bounces and claps. "That's so, *so* nice to hear. Been here just a couple hours and already you're learning so much. You be sure to tell Jeff about it when he returns. Tell him *just like that*, okay, sweetie?"

"Okay," Lilith agrees, folding her hands primly on her lap. "We were just talking about our lives and regretting our past decisions. We could keep doing that while you handle other issues."

"Oh, now," Mrs. Mitchell says, "that won't be necessary. Y'all didn't come here to talk all day. Y'all came here to *help*! In just a moment, we'll get ready for the lunch crew."

Rex mutters, but Mrs. Mitchell doesn't seem to hear it.

"Should we wait here until you're ready for us?" Lilith asks.

"That'd be lovely, dear," Mrs. Mitchell says. "Give you more time to bond, too." She winks. "I'll be back in a jiffy. Just going to pop into the kitchen and grab some hairnets for y'all." Her squeaky steps echo down the hall.

"That was amazing, Lily," Wes says, leaning toward her. "It proves how much we need you."

Lilith crosses her arms and taps her foot on the floor.

"I'm serious," Wes says. "What you did just there? How did

you know what to say to get her to do exactly what we needed her to do?"

Even though her parents rarely observe their parents' traditions, they do embrace the constant flow of elderly relatives, even if it is only for the free babysitting. Grandparents, great uncles, and cousins always are around, and Lilith is at expert level at figuring out what they want to hear before grandparently interest turns into prying.

Lilith boosts her chin up, away from Wes.

"The rest of us wouldn't have been able to pull that off. Am I right, guys?" He glances at the others.

"I guess so," Ally mutters.

"Um, sure," Jason says.

Wes tilts his head toward Rex. She grimaces but says, "Yeah, it was great."

Lilith shrugs, a tiny jerk of her shoulders. She struggles to hide a smile.

"What we need for our plan to work is an actress," Wes says. "The rest of us would never be able to do it. And think about it. This is a great role!"

Slowly Lilith's eyes glide back to Wes's, aware that he's playing her just as expertly as she did Mrs. Mitchell. Still, he has a point. "Well, it's true that the rest of you wouldn't be able to improvise the way I can."

"Absolutely," Wes agrees. "We need someone who will convince TBN she wants your bracelet and who's skilled enough to make it accessible to her."

Lilith taps her foot a couple more times. "Do you promise that we'll get the bracelet back? It's a family heirloom."

"I promise."

Lilith uncrosses her arms. "Fine, I'll go along with the plan. But I'm in charge."

"No," Wes says, "it's my plan."

"No," Rex counters, her voice hard. "*I'm* in charge. This is my deal, not any of yours."

"Either I'm in charge or I'm not doing it." Lilith puts her hands on her hips, making sure the bracelet is facing outward.

Wes turns toward Rex, an eyebrow raised, waiting for her response.

"Whatever," Rex growls. "If it makes Drama Queen feel better about herself to think she's in charge, fine. She's in charge."

Lilith smiles. "Everyone, follow my lead."

10:24 a.m.

JASON "The Nobody"

Mrs. Mitchell comes back with five hairnets and white aprons. *It's official,* Jason thinks as Ally tucks her hair back into the hairnet. *No one looks good in a hairnet.*

"All righty now," Mrs. Mitchell says as they tie their aprons around their waists. "Let's all pair up."

Wes sidesteps toward Rex. Jason falls in line next to Ally. Mrs. Mitchell goes down the line. "Wes, you're one. Rex is two. Ally one. Jason two. Lilith one. Ones clear trays. Twos serve residents in the food line."

Everyone groans.

"It's only ten thirty," Rex points out.

"Oh, we better hurry then! The residents will be lining up. We start serving at ten forty-five." Mrs. Mitchell beckons them to follow her down the hall. "The regular staff is going to love having a little break!"

"So we get back to the plan after lunch?" Jason whispers to the group.

Rex grits her teeth. "I guess."

Wes nods. "Will TBN be around the cafeteria?"

Rex shrugs. "I don't know. I'd guess she'll be bringing residents there to eat."

"Sounds like a good time to nab a thing or two," Ally muses.

Lilith nods. "Okay, so Wes and Ally, keep an eye on the entrance and exits. When TBN enters, laugh—loudly—so we"—she points to Jason, Rex, and back to herself—"know when it's time to act. I'll get into place. When it starts getting real, Jason, you'll need to skip out on the food line and trail her with your phone, recording what happens."

"What about me?" Rex asks.

"You take over clearing trays." Lilith's eyebrows scrunch in an *isn't-it-obvious* way.

"And serving?" Rex growls. "For the whole cafeteria?"

Lilith shrugs. "Improvise." She daintily trots toward Mrs. Mitchell. "Oh, Mrs. Mitchell," she sing-songs. "These hairnets are so convenient!"

10:28 a.m.

WES "The Flirt"

Wes walks beside Ally.

"What's up?" he asks her. "You're seriously glaring at Lilith."

Ally shrugs and looks away. Lilith and Ally, now that Wes thought about it, were about as different as any two people could be. Where Lilith was posh and shining, Ally was all straight lines and grit.

"I guess I get it," Wes whispers to Ally. "She's kind of tough to take."

Ally nods. "She looks like she belongs on the top floor of a dollhouse, in a pink bedroom with a white canopy bed. Like when someone meets her, they should be given a little plastic comb to run through her shiny hair."

Wes muffles his laugh with his hand. Ahead of them, Lilith seems to glide rather than walk next to Mrs. Mitchell's *bounce, bounce, bounce* steps.

"About this tray clearing," Lilith says, "I'm not going to scrape dirty dishes. I have misophonia—fear of disgusting sounds. I could become ill, and I'm sure you don't want that."

"Miso—" Mrs. Mitchell echoes.

"Misophonia," Lilith responds. "It's a medical condition."

"And my brother is aware of your condition?" Mrs. Mitchell asks.

"Of course," Lilith responds. "I can't believe Mr. Hardy hasn't shared our medical restrictions with you! That seems like such a lapse in care."

Mrs. Mitchell nods, her cheeks wobbling with the force of it. "I pride myself in knowing residents' restrictions." She makes a tutting sound with her tongue. "The moment their health status changes, I demand to know. That way I can make any necessary changes on my end—you know, transferring them to other floors and whatnot—right away. I can't believe my brother wouldn't mention your miso . . . messio . . ."

"Misophonia." Lilith smiles. "So, no plate scraping?"

"Of course not, dear," Mrs. Mitchell says. "How about we station one of the others by the trash cans, so they can take care of that job?"

Ally groans.

"You've got to admit, she's got skills," Wes says.

Ally raises an eyebrow.

"You disagree?"

"A five-minute mile is impressive," Ally says. "*She* passed out—for real, passed out—after a thirteen-minute mile in gym class."

Wes laughs again. "Yeah, but I bet it was the loveliest fainting spell ever." He puts his head to his forehead and pretends to swoon. "Ally," Wes says, "you're in, right? I mean, you've been pretty quiet. We can count on you?" He's matching her long-legged pace down the hall toward the cafeteria. His dark eyes watch hers.

"Stop looking at me like that," she whispers.

"Like what?" Wes's step slows.

"Like I'm weak." Two red circles flame on her face and her jaw clenches.

"I wasn't saying—"

"I'm in, okay?"

"Okay," Wes says, trying to figure out where he went wrong. "You don't talk much, do you?"

"That again?"

"What?" Wes tilts his head at the strange girl.

"Asking me if I can talk. You did that in first grade." Wes's eyes crinkle as he tries to remember. Finally, he does. He and Ally had been paired for a stupid math project, sorting plastic pieces. Wes had turned the little dinosaurs into a herd, making the squares a fence around them. Ally had silently counted the sets and wrote the numbers on their paper while he played. *Do you even know how to talk?* he had asked. She had stomped on his T. rex herd and refused to work with him. He hadn't even said it in a mean way. He really didn't know. He had *wanted* to know. Yet here she was, carrying that memory like a piece of chewed-up bubblegum stuck under a desk. "Seriously? You're still angry about *first* grade?"

Ally's chin pops up. "I'm not *angry*. I just remember it."

"You have trouble letting things go, huh?" Wes winces as something flickers across Ally's face, like she's watching a catalog of hurts flash by.

"I know how to talk," Ally blurts.

After a too-long pause, Wes says, again not in a mean way, "Okay. Good. That's going to be helpful. Great."

Outside the cafeteria door, the lunch lineup of wheelchairs and walkers winds around the corner.

"I thought lunch wasn't being served until ten forty-five?" Wes asks, checking his phone for the time. It is ten thirty-two.

"That's right," Mrs. Mitchell calls. "Residents like to line up early, especially when we have a favorite on the menu like today."

"Chicken nuggets?" Wes asks. "Chicken nuggets draw a crowd in middle school."

"Nope, something even better today!" Mrs. Mitchell says. "Tuna casserole!"

Mrs. Mitchell opens the cafeteria door, releasing a cloud of fish-scented air.

"Mmm, tuna casserole," says a little woman in a purple pantsuit.

"Mmm," Wes echoes with a little shudder. The woman in the purple pantsuit winks at him, beckoning Wes toward her with fingers covered in heavy rings. She presses a piece of butterscotch hard candy into his palm. "Our secret," she whispers.

"Puke," Rex mutters.

Wes winks back at the old woman, unwraps the candy, and pops it in his mouth.

"How does he do that?" Rex asks, and Ally shakes her head.

Wes is grinning past Ally to a white-haired man heading in the opposite direction. "Hubert!" says Wes, holding out his arm to shake the old man's hand.

Hubert motions for a high five instead. An awkward back and forth follows, as Wes tries to turn the handshake into a fist bump and as Hubert grabs Wes's fist for a handshake. Wes laughs a little as he reaches and grabs Hubert's arm with his other hand, holding it in place so he can slip into a handshake at last.

"Where are you headed? The cafeteria's this way." Wes points ahead. "As Tray Clearer, I could pull a few strings, sneak you to the head of the line. Get that tuna casserole while it's hot!"

Hubert clears his throat. "You're a good boy, Wes. I have a little, um, thing to do before lunch, though." Under his breath, he adds, "Didn't know it was tuna casserole day."

"S'okay," Wes says. He glances behind him, scanning the growing line of residents waiting for the door to open. "I'll look for Grace. Save a seat for you next to her. Should I let her know you'll be there soon?"

"No!" Hubert answers, his voice suddenly harsh. "No," he adds a little softer. "That won't be necessary. Don't, um . . . don't mention that you saw me." His cheeks turn pink. "I, ah, I've got to go take a nap. Grace . . . knows I'm taking a nap. Knows I'm tired." Hubert forces a yawn.

The older man limps down the hall at a faster clip than before, beelining for the elevator.

"Huh," Ally says.

"What?" Wes asks.

"It's just, even *I* can tell he's lying. And I'm really bad at telling when people are lying."

Wes stands on tiptoe, watching Hubert.

"Fourth floor, please," the old man says to another resident who is standing by the buttons in the elevator.

"Wasn't Hubert's room on this level?" Wes asks. "Why would he be going to the fourth floor for a nap?"

Rex pushes by Wes. "Give the man his space. You don't have to be nosing around in everyone's business."

"It's just weird. Why would he be lying?"

Rex turns back with a smirk. "Starting to doubt true love, Ding?"

"Never!" Wes calls, cupping his hands around his mouth so Rex could hear him as she disappears into the cafeteria, Jason just behind her.

Wes then notices Ally jump as her hair is rustled by the frail-looking old woman, Opal. The woman stretches her hand to pat Ally's poufy bun again, her mouth popping open and closed with each bounce of her hand. Ally grimaces.

Wes nudges her side. *Say something*, he mouths.

But before Ally can, Lilith strides toward them. Opal retreats back to the line. "Look," Lilith says, "I scoped out the cafeteria. If you and Ally stick to this main entrance, I'll stand guard at the opposite side, working the crowd for details about TBN. Remember your signal. Remember the plan." She turns, her shoes clicking across the floor.

Wes laughs. "She's kind of scary, isn't she?"

Ally nods, her eyes on Opal.

10:35 a.m.

JASON "The Nobody"

"Any chance this will actually work?" Rex asks Jason as they pass through the cafeteria to the serving station.

He shrugs. "Lilith takes this acting stuff super seriously. Like, *super* seriously."

"What have I got to lose?" Rex mutters. Jason flashes a quick smile her way. "Huh," Rex adds.

"What?" Jason pats at the hairnet.

"You have pretty eyes. They're sort of gray."

"Oh. I know." Jason feels his face flame again and mentally swears at his pale complexion and the way it constantly showcases his discomfort.

"Don't get weird about it." Rex grins. "Just maybe look up once in a while. Get your hair out of your face now and then. Talk—about yourself—occasionally. Might help with the Ally situation."

"Ally situation?" Jason shakes his head. "There's no Ally situation."

Rex winks as she strides ahead of Jason. "Exactly."

They take their positions behind the counter, breathing in the tuna casserole air as they scoop servings onto trays. Jason tries not to notice how the old people lick their lips waiting for the plop of canned fish and noodles.

"You know, the cherry on top of this cat food sundae is counting on Drama Queen and the Scooby-Doo crew to finally catch TBN," Rex hisses.

"Do you even know TBN's real name?" Jason asks.

Rex shrugs. "It's too cutesy to say. Starts with a *c*."

"So, I'm Picasso. Lilith is Drama Queen. Ally is Sports Barbie. Wes is ..."

"Ding." Rex smirks.

"What's your problem with real names?"

Rex swallows. "They're dumb. I mean, a name is just a word, right? And that word is supposed to represent a person. But how could a whole person be represented by one word, used by everyone, even though each of us is totally different to everyone else?"

Jason nods, staring at the spatula in his hand. Slowly, he says,

"*Or* using someone's name out loud makes a person real, harder to shake."

"You're a little stingy with the peaches, Picasso," she says as if he hadn't spoken.

"Yeah, Picasso," says the resident reaching for a just-filled peach cup. "More juice!" The man takes the cup and sips at the juice, glaring at Jason.

Jason fills the next cup with extra juice and hands it to the man. Then he sucks in a breath like he's about to dive into a swimming pool. "When I'm old," he finally says, "I'm going to only eat candy. Not the hard stuff, either. Chocolate. Caramel. Toffee. I'm going to buy it in giant bags and have it all over the place. My grandchildren and great-grandchildren will have contests with me to see who can eat the most. And I'll always win."

"Dream big," says Rex, dispensing another plop of tuna casserole onto a tray.

Jason looks out into the cafeteria. Lilith is flitting around the room, giggling and chatting with the residents. Wes and Ally are by the main entrance, once in a while carting trays to the trash cans but mostly staring out the doors, most likely on the lookout for TBN.

Jason feels Rex's eyes on him. His cheeks feel flushed, but there isn't anything he can do about it. Rex told him to share more about himself, but he guesses she didn't mean for him to share anything with her. His eyes slide to the left and he sees something unravel on Rex's face. Great. Now impenetrable Rex is feeling sorry for him. *This is why it's better to be invisible*, he thinks.

"You know, Picasso, this is just one day," she says. "At school, everyone's going to go back to their own little circles and never talk to us again."

Jason nods.

"Also, your dream sounds noisy—all that chewing. All those grandkids and great-grandkids." She's smiling down at the tuna casserole while she talks.

Jason laughs. "It's just me and my parents now. If I ever have kids, I'm having a dozen of them. Spread out the expectations a little so if one's a loser, it's not such a big deal."

"You're not a loser." The words rush out of Rex's mouth.

Jason sort of nods, not looking at her. Clearing his throat, he says, "What about you?"

Rex snorts. "I think the consensus is mostly loser. Ask anyone."

"No, no," Jason blurts. "Not that. You're not . . ." He clears his throat. "I mean what about you when you're old? What do you want to do? You know, what do you want to *be* when you're an adult?"

Rex huffs out of her nose. The next scoop of tuna slaps down on the tray with a little too much force. "My brother asked me that once," she whispers. Jason knows better than to look at her. He tries not to breathe. Rex never talks about her brother. "I was, I don't know, three, maybe. He was thirteen."

"Our age," Jason prompts when her voice trails off.

"Yeah. He was trying to figure out which courses to pick for high school. I don't really remember this, you know. But Aug—my brother—he told it so many times, it feels like I do."

Jason nods. Rex grinds her teeth, her jaw flexing, and Jason is sure she isn't going to say anymore. But then, super quietly, she does. "I was sitting next to him. Mama used to say I treated him like he was my armchair, like he sort of just molded around me— his arm was like my seat belt, I guess."

Rex's eyes are unfocused and Jason knows she's seeing some-thing entirely internal as the memory unfolds. She isn't hearing the old people shuffling down the line for their lunch; it is her brother's voice she's tuned into. Maybe she even smells him over the fishy scent of the cafeteria.

Jason once tried to sketch memory as if it were a real thing. He had been ransacking his mind for a moment when his dad hadn't been disappointed in him, when being next to each other had been easy. He had drawn memory as a blanket, a thin fabric of once-upon-a-times and don't-ever-forgets covering something bright and glowing—a soul, maybe—with rips where kids forgot things like the rumble of a person's voice when your head rests on their chest or the smell of them when their arm is wrapped around you.

Rex's voice is so soft, Jason leans closer to hear her. "He asked me, 'What are you going to be when you grow up, T. rex?'"

"What did you say?"

Rex smirks. "Bigger."

Jason snorts, which makes Rex laugh. When she composes herself, she says, "August had laughed so hard a neighbor had knocked on the wall between our apartments." She shakes her head. "That's not even really right. He didn't just laugh. He exploded, like the sound erupted out and through him. I think he laughed loud enough that a picture fell off the wall."

"You said his name," Jason says without thinking. "August. You said his name."

Rex winces. The silence between them, even in a cafeteria humming with sounds, is painful.

"Rex?" Jason is staring at her, his eyes searching.

Finally working loose her jaw, she mutters, "Know what I'm going to be when I grow up, Picasso? Nothing. I'm not going to be anything."

Jason opens his mouth and Rex groans. "*Why* did I tell you to talk today, Picasso?"

But the resident in front of them interrupts, asking for a corner piece of casserole. Rex scoops it onto the tray just as Jason spots TBN. She's walking into the cafeteria, guiding Opal.

He forces out a laugh. But it's like his brain doesn't even know what a laugh is, like trying to produce the right sound is like trying to recreate a Jackson Pollock piece with a No. 2 pencil. He tries again, a little louder.

"Whoa," Rex gasps and slaps him hard between the shoulder blades. *She thinks I'm choking*, he realizes. Still, he can only manage the same guttural gasp, his mouth stretched wide and eyes huge. He points toward the back of the cafeteria. Rex follows his pointing finger, just as a strangling cat sound erupts from another corner. Rex turns her head toward the sound—it's Ally, and she's pointing in the same direction as Jason. Realization blooms across Rex's face. "You and Sports Barbie are trying to *laugh*. You're both terrible at it."

Jason goes up on his toes, dropping the spoon of peach slices onto the tray with a rattle. He scans the entrances. TBN is by the back entrance, hovering over Opal.

"TBN was sneaking in that old lady's room earlier!" Rex hisses.

TBN's whispering something in the old lady's ear. Then she stands and shoves something small and sparkly into her pocket.

11:00 a.m.

ⅬILITH "The Drama Queen"

Lilith struggles to keep a grimace off her face as Ally's and Jason's croak-like laughs assault the cafeteria. TBN must be nearby; the sound of their fake laughing is brutal. Few people realize how much practice goes into a natural-sounding laugh. Lilith scans the room for the nurse then spots her in the back of the cafeteria, leaning over a woman with fluffy white hair.

"Aren't you here to see Agnes?" asks a thin, tailored black woman sitting just in front of where Lilith has positioned herself. She's wearing a neat purple pantsuit and a string of pearls and is taking pecks of casserole from her spoon. A small pile of crinkled-up butterscotch candy wrappers are beside her tray.

Lilith shakes her head. "No, I'm here on my own."

"Oh, that's too bad," says the woman, sucking on one of the candies. "Agnes has the best stories."

Lilith's attention is momentarily pulled from TBN. "Are there several Agneses here?"

The woman softly laughs. "No, no. Only one Agnes. Did she tell you about the oatmeal?"

"Yes, I *know* Agnes loves her oatmeal." Lilith rolls her eyes and refocuses on TBN. "Excuse me, I have to speak to that nurse."

The little woman shudders. "Wouldn't you rather find Agnes?"

Lilith tilts her chin toward the woman. "You don't like TBN?"

"Who now?" the woman murmurs, her eyes narrowing as she, too, watches the nurse.

"Never mind," Lilith says as Wes gestures across the cafeteria. Who knew what signal he was trying to make—his mouth flailing, his fingertips going from his eyes to hers and then to TBN. Lilith allows herself a moment to feel the pain of knowing Wes will never star next to her onstage despite the adorableness of his dimple and his flawless complexion. She presses a hand to her heart and shakes her head.

"Oh, would you look at that cool drink of water?" the older woman says. Lilith swivels her head. The woman is transformed, somehow, her eyes wide and blinking rapidly. A wide smile spreads across her face as she gazes at Wes. The woman pats her cheeks. "Travis is here. Today's the day. I just know it. He's going to ask me to prom. I just know it!"

"What? You mean Wes?"

He must've heard his name because Wes grins in their direction. And then, weirdly, he *winks* at the old woman.

"That's my Travis. Lord above, he's looking my way!" The woman giggles behind her hand like a girl. "How do I look?" she asks Lilith, smoothing her hair with her hands.

"Um, great." The woman is beautiful, Lilith admits. Her dark skin isn't really wrinkled, just a little creased by the eyes and around her mouth. Her eyes are bright, somehow, as if she were a teenager just a smidgen older than Lilith.

"I'm going in," the woman says, and pushes up from her seat.

"Going in?" Lilith echoes.

"To get me a prom date," the woman replies.

"Wait!" Lilith says. She still had to get over to TBN, talk about her bracelet, and leave it somewhere obvious for TBN to steal. Then Wes and Ally had to trail TBN to her hiding place while Rex and Jason made sure Mr. Hardy and Mrs. Mitchell were distracted. After that, Lilith would retrieve all of the missing jewelry and be universally admired for her hard work in single-handedly leading the effort to solve the mystery.

But if Wes is off playing along with this old lady's prom dreams, how could he help them nab TBN? Lilith sighs again as

Wes turns on his heel and heads toward the door in the opposite direction of TBN, trailing a tall old man with white hair passing by the open doors instead of focusing on his *one job*. The little woman in the purple pantsuit is just behind him.

The show must go on. If Ranveer Singh could fall from a platform, land on his face, get a few stitches, and jump right back to dancing without delaying the *Gunday* production, Lilith Bhat could bring down this nurse with or without Wes.

She takes a deep breath and plucks a pea from the old woman's abandoned tray. Squinting toward Ally—who finally has stopped her fake cackle to stare at the purple pantsuit lady pushing another woman using a walker out of her way—Lilith takes aim. *Plunk!* The pea hits Ally in the forehead.

Ally rubs at the spot and looks around. Lilith pelts her with another pea. Finally, Ally sees Lilith, who throws up her hands in a *come on, already!* sort of way and then beckons her to follow as she turns toward TBN.

11:00 a.m.

JASON "The Nobody"

"I get it, I get it," Rex says. "TBN is here. Stop trying to laugh. Please."

But before he can rearrange his face into something normal, Mrs. Mitchell rushes into the room, hastily cramming her hair up into a net. "Oh, dear, you have the messatophia, don't you? Oh, dear! Oh, dear!" She grabs Jason around the shoulders. "We'll get you to the nurse, darling! Don't you worry!"

"I think he's fine," Rex tries to sputter, but before she can finish, Jason starts croaking again. "Picasso, you okay?"

Mrs. Mitchell slips her arm under Jason's and half leads, half pulls him out of the food service area and toward the exit.

"Picasso!" Rex calls again. Jason, still croaking, looks back over Mrs. Mitchell's shoulder and pops a thumbs-up in Rex's direction. Rex smirks and picks up the spatula. "Got this covered," she calls to Mrs. Mitchell. "I think he's going to need some water or something."

But Mrs. Mitchell is barely listening, leading Jason out into the hall. "I can't believe Frank wouldn't tell me all of y'alls issues and troubles. There you are, choking like a cat on a hairball, right over the residents' lunch!"

He clears his throat, about to tell Mrs. Mitchell that he's better (now that he's out of the cafeteria and in position to trail TBN, should Lilith manage to lay the bait as planned), but then Wes rushes by, knocking into Mrs. Mitchell and continuing on down the hall.

"Where are you going, young man?" Mrs. Mitchell twists after Wes, yanking Jason with her. Wes is trailing Hubert. And Hubert is at the end of the hall now, embracing a much younger woman. Hubert's taller than the woman and whispering something in her ear. The woman reaches up and pats his cheek. *Whoa.*

Jason clears his throat. "I'm feeling much better now."

"The nurse should check you out," says Mrs. Mitchell, but just then they are knocked again, this time by a petite woman in a purple pantsuit.

"Travis! Oh, Travis!" the woman calls.

Mrs. Mitchell drops her grip on Jason. "What in the world is going on?" she stammers, then calls out to the woman: "Judith, what are you up to?" She throws up her arms. "Whole place is going wild! Go get yourself some water or something," she says to Jason, and trudges after the purple pantsuit woman. "Judith! *Judith!*"

"I can't slow down!" the woman calls. "Travis is getting away!"

"Judith, you get back here right now!" Mrs. Mitchell yells.

Judith turns, sticks her tongue out at Mrs. Mitchell, and shouts, "You're not gonna keep me from going to my prom, Mama! I'm going shopping! Get me a dress!" She scuttles into the open elevator and disappears behind the doors.

Mrs. Mitchell pulls a walkie-talkie from its clip at her waist-line. "I'm going to need staff members at the elevator doors on each floor. Judith thinks she's going to prom again." She sighs, and when she turns back toward Jason her face is splotchy. "I *told* them she needed to be in the dementia ward. We have to *move* patients when they start to lose their faculties or we end up with visiting middle school delinquents getting hit on by the elderly. But *nooo!* Nurses want to keep their patients, have them stay put in their care. *Give 'em time.* Time for what? *Prom?*"

Jason mumbles, "We're not delinquents."

"And speaking of delinquents, *where is my brother?*" Mrs. Mitchell throws her arms up again, forcing them down with a slapping sound on her thighs. "Typical," she says to no one in particular as she marches after Judith. "Everyone leaving me to clean up their messes!"

As Mrs. Mitchell stomps toward the elevator, Jason's eyes the cafeteria—where Lilith, Ally, and Rex are waiting for him to do his part—and then Wes, who has disappeared around the corner. Jason throws up his arms like Mrs. Mitchell, then darts down the hall after Wes.

11:04 a.m.

WES "The Flirt"

What is it that his mom always says? Oh, yeah: *Don't insert yourself into conversations where you aren't invited.*

She had picked up that line from the therapist she had seen during the divorce. Or the "uncoupling," as she phrased it after a month or so of therapy. But his mom and dad weren't "uncoupled." No one with kids is ever "uncoupled," not to the kids anyway. Each parent always will be one half of a complete set. And the kid is the sticky thing that keeps them together.

Yet, *don't insert yourself* is what goes through his mind as he trots down the hall after Hubert and the pretty, *much* younger woman he's got his arm wrapped around. Wes's nostrils flare as he follows the old man who had so clearly been lying to him an hour earlier and who had seemed so in love with Grace just that morning. *Am I really seeing this?*

Hubert and the woman pause in front of the main doors. Again, Hubert kisses the woman on the cheek. She wraps her arms around him.

Wes stops, his feet suddenly dragging as if going through mud. *Don't insert yourself.* But in the space of a breath—just the time it took for the younger woman to tuck her forehead against Hubert's neck for a moment—Wes remembers back months and years and maybe even a decade, to all the times he had been the one in the middle—the one who suddenly needed a drink of water in the middle of the night because he knew his footsteps down the stairs in the dark would be the only way they'd stop fighting; the one who brought home trophies and certificates and anything that would lead to celebrating over a pizza, together as a family; the one who could charm his mom into smiling and his dad into dropping the grudge. *Don't insert yourself.* Sometimes you didn't have a choice. You're in the middle.

And maybe this is different—maybe whatever Hubert is doing, whatever he's done to Grace—should mean nothing to Wes. But he also didn't choose Hubert to be his senior today. Yet he is. And whether either of them wants it, Wes is inserted right smack in the middle once again.

Starting to doubt true love, Ding?

Wes walks toward the couple just as they pull apart from their embrace. "When are you going to tell Grace?" the woman asks. "She has a right to know."

"Yeah, Hubert," Wes finds himself saying. "When are you going to tell Grace?"

Both of them turn toward Wes, Hubert's face a brilliant red, the woman's pretty face puckering. Slowly, they step apart.

"Who's this?" the woman asks.

Wes glares at her but doesn't answer.

Hubert clears his throat. "Wes, this has nothing to do with you. This is a family matter."

A mean chuckle escapes Wes's mouth. "Seems like it has an awful lot to do with Grace, though, doesn't it?"

"He's right," the woman says quietly, looking at her feet.

Wes groans as the woman kisses Hubert on the cheek again. "Really?" He shakes his head, but the woman keeps her eyes on Hubert.

"You have to tell her. And soon."

Hubert rakes his hand over his face. "Why are you both so intent on me breaking her heart?"

Wes crosses his arms. "As if you haven't already. She just doesn't know it yet." He swallows hard, but the painful lump in his throat doesn't shift. For a moment, he is flooded with too many memories of two different women crying. First, his mom, who hadn't cried when she found out Dad had moved in with someone else; she cried when she found out Wes had known about it and hadn't told her. Second, a different woman but one whose cries wouldn't stop echoing alongside his mom's. Wes squishes shut his eyes to push away the memory of the last day of school, the one that had led to spending the day at Northbrook Retirement Village.

"You just need to own up to it, man," Wes chokes out to Hubert. "You just need to tell her and let her get on with her life."

And for some reason, for some stupid reason that doesn't make any sense to him, Wes begins to shake. Then suddenly Wes realizes Jason has crept up behind him. Maybe crept isn't the right word. Maybe Jason just walked in that quiet way of his while Wes was too busy shaking, and maybe even almost crying, to notice. But there he is, his head hanging low with his hair across his face, his hands shoved into his pockets. Jason's just standing there. Just being there. And for some reason, that makes Wes stop shaking.

Hubert's big shoulders rise and fall with a shudder. The other woman reaches out to Wes, as if to pat his shoulder, but he steps away from her, making Jason side step, too. The woman's arm falls to her side.

"Take the boy's advice. Tell her." The woman pushes her purse strap back up from where it had slid down her shoulder. "I'll call you tonight." She turns away, but glances back over her shoulder.

"I love you, Dad."

"Dad?" Wes echoes. "Wait. What?"

And now that both Hubert and the woman share the same puckered-up confused face, Wes can see it—the family resemblance. And suddenly the embrace that triggered all of this melts into just a hug. And the kisses were just pecks on the cheek. And the secret is something else entirely.

Hubert's mouth pops open as he stares at Wes. The woman sucks in her breath. And then both erupt, laughter shooting out and over them in the same way, as if laughter is genetic. Between gasps, Hubert chokes out, "Wes, I'd like you to meet my daughter, Jenna."

Jenna, still quaking, holds out her hand. Numbly, Wes shakes it. "I needed that laugh, thank you, Wes." She then waves to her dad and strides out the door.

"What do you need to tell Grace, then?" Wes asks.

Hubert's face clouds immediately. "It's a family matter." Shoulders slumping, he turns back down the hall.

"Oh, man. I'm sorry, Wes," Jason whispers.

"Sorry about what?"

But Jason simply watches Hubert walk away.

"What?" Wes asks again.

Jason pulls his hand through his hair before meeting Wes's eyes.

How did this kid figure out what was going on when I'm still clueless? Wes thinks. But before he can ask Jason, a nurse cuts between them, holding a walkie-talkie to her ear. Her voice is low as she says, "We have a patient who needs transfer up to hospice."

And that's when it hits Wes. Northbrook, despite all of its relationships and its cafeteria and its principal-like Mrs. Mitchell, isn't a school. It isn't a place where the residents just hang out. It's a place for people to go when they can't live by themselves. It's a place for people to go to finish their lives. It is a place for people who are dying—even people who just got married.

"Sorry, man," Jason says again.

Wes shakes his head, and then follows Jason back toward the cafeteria.

"Psst!" A thin arm and hand shoots out from behind a big fake ornamental tree. A scrap of paper is clutched in the fingers. Without thinking Wes reaches for it. It's a phone number written in shaky print.

"Call me about prom, Travis!" Wes squints through the branches and sees a small face. "I have to go. My mom's after me."

Then the woman, still holding the tree as cover, backs down the hall.

Don't insert yourself, Wes reminds himself, and catches up to Jason.

11:13 a.m.

LILITH "The Drama Queen"

Ha! Lilith doesn't bother stifling her laugh when a second pea slams Ally right between the eyes with an overly cooked *splat*. Sure, Ally might be the pitcher for the softball team but that doesn't mean Lilith can't give her a little competition if she desires. Which she doesn't.

Ally rubs at the sticky spot and makes her way toward Lilith. Her face, which could be so pretty with a little accentuation of the cheekbones and an artful eyebrow shaping, is screwed up in a *why-am-I-doing-this* expression. Lilith reads her like she's a font on a typed page. It's a gift she has—tapping into what other people are thinking. People have no idea how many expressions float across their face, clear as words in a script. Most people don't bother reading them, but Lilith can't stop doing so, even when she doesn't want to, even when what she reads tugs at something in her chest. And Ally's face is crystal clear. She's thinking she doesn't care—like none of them are her friends.

But Lilith has seen Ally's so-called friends. Just like the cast around Lilith's table shifts with every play or project she leads, Ally's table changes with sports seasons. *Ally probably only sees uniforms, not faces when she thinks of friends.* It's not a smug thought. If anything, it stirs up something else in Lilith's chest. Something a lot like understanding.

Ally moves toward Lilith, who nods. *Show's on.* Suddenly, Lilith is flitting around the room like a bumblebee—smiling at residents, waving to others (showing off her bracelet, of course)—and heading right toward TBN and Opal.

"Come on," Lilith mouths to Ally.

But Ally is stuck, trying to scoot past two women who are blocking her path to Lilith with their chairs. Just as Ally begins to backtrack and move around the table in the opposite direction, one of the ladies calls out, "Oh, miss! Miss! Would you take our trays for us?"

The other woman nods. The one on the left wears a red hat as big as a sunbonnet and the one on the right is also wearing a red hat, but hers is small and round against her head. The one with the bonnet is the one speaking. She leans forward to get Ally's attention and now is shifting side to side as she piles the trays with about thirty crumpled napkins in a mountain on top. Meanwhile, the second lady rolls back and forth in her seat to avoid getting swatted by the bonnet.

Ally nods and picks up the trays while Lilith tries not to groan out loud. In one voice, the ladies say, "Thank you, dear!" and then go back to their whispering and laughing. Ally dumps the food and stacks the trays back near the kitchen.

Three more times on her way toward Lilith, Ally is flagged down to clear trays. Once Lilith glances her way and mouths *hurry up!* Ally holds the trays and arches an eyebrow.

But Ally could totally move faster. Be a bit speedier on clearing the trays. Be her usual pushing-to-the-limits self.

Lilith is now standing at the table where TBN is helping Opal spread out her napkin over her lap. She's opening a container of something—pudding, by the look of it—for the old woman.

Ally scrapes clear the same tray again and again. Every time she seems ready to stack it with the other trays, she glances over at Opal, shudders a little, and gives the tray an extra scrape.

Whatever. Time to step up the performance, Lilith tells herself. She's leans her back against the table, talking to residents at the full table in front of her. "Well," she says in a loud, carrying voice, "would any of you like some help? I'd be glad to do it. I just *love* helping the elderly!"

"Who are you calling elderly?" says an old man with a gruff voice.

Lilith giggles. Only, unlike *some people*, Lilith's makes her laugh sound natural. "My grandmother taught me how important it is to help others. Yeah," she says, twisting the arm with the bracelet so it glimmers in the florescent lights, "Dida's the one who gave me this gold bracelet. She told me that I should always remember her when I wear it—remember how valuable I am. *Just like this bracelet is valuable.* Just wear it, she said." Lilith cradles her braceleted arm against her chest. "Wear it and remember my name."

She catches Ally wincing. It's possible she's overdoing it. But the residents just nod. "What's her name?" a bald man with a few fuzzy strands of hair asks. He's shoveling casserole onto his fork, but not looking at the plate.

Lilith is quiet for too long. *Bharati*, she thinks. *Bharati.* But she can't bring herself to say the name.

"What's her name?" another person at the table repeats.

"Her name?" Lilith repeats.

"Yeah. Your grandmother's name."

"Oh," Lilith says. She swallows down what she knows would come next if she answered truthfully—their foreheads would pucker; they'd say things like how it's "exotic" or "different."

They'd smile too big and then get too quiet.

"Her name is Becky," Lilith snaps.

"That's my granddaughter's name!" The old man tries to scoop up more casserole and misses it entirely, bringing an empty fork to his mouth. The woman next to him guides his hand to the mound of food, and he mutters something about minding her own business.

Lilith doesn't respond but glances behind her at TBN, who unwraps a straw and adds it to Opal's cup.

"Frank, need any help with dinner?" TBN asks. To Lilith, she says, "Macular degeneration. He's blind."

"Oh," Lilith says, and twirls the bracelet around her wrist. To Frank, Lilith says, "It's gold. Very nice quality. I think she probably got it in India."

Frank nods. "Becky doesn't wear a lot of jewelry. She sings, though. Her voice is pretty, even when she's just talking. Just like yours."

"Well, I am a fantastic singer. Everyone says so."

Lilith hears Ally sigh but ignores her.

"Becky's going to visit me soon. She says so every time she calls. 'Soon,' she says. 'Soon I'll make it out there.'" The old man nods and the woman next to him pats his arm. Again he mutters under his breath and shakes off her hand.

"Where does she live?" Lilith asks.

"Montana," Frank says. "Maybe I'll go there myself this summer. When my eyes get better."

"Can that happen?" Lilith asks. "Your eyes, I mean. Can they get better?"

TBN clears her throat. She shakes her head at Lilith.

Frank doesn't seem to have heard Lilith's question. He scoops up more tuna casserole.

"Who needs help?" Lilith asks. With that, she turns toward the table where Opal is sitting and slips off her bracelet. "I'll just put this valuable bracelet here so I can help. It's so precious to my family. They'd hate if I mucked it up with tuna casserole."

Lilith turns away again, stretches out her arm behind her, and, without looking, plunks the bracelet on the table in front of TBN. And that's when she realizes the plan is not going to work.

TBN isn't even looking at the bracelet. She's pushing through residents to get to the red hat ladies, who seem to be having some sort of emergency. Wide brim red hat lady is standing with her arms outstretched. "Now! Now!" she says. Small red hat lady, about twenty pounds heavier and three inches taller than her friend, stands on top of her chair with her back to wide brim red hat lady. "Now?" she asks.

Her friend shouts, "Now!"

Still rushing across the room, TBN bellows, "No! Don't do it! Don't do it!"

The entire cafeteria turns—some half standing, some gasping, some chuckling—toward the red hat pair.

"It's a trust fall," Ally gasps.

"A what?" Lilith scrunches her face at not knowing what's going on.

"We had to do them in cross country at a team-building session last year." Ally bites her lip. "I hid in the bathroom, hoping no one would notice I left."

"Did they?"

Ally glares at Lilith.

"Guess that answers that."

Small red hat lady crosses her arms over her chest and falls backward toward her friend's outstretched arms.

TBN, fast as any linebacker, rushes through the crowd, lunging forward and intercepting the falling small red hat lady just before she falls into wide brim red hat lady. Grunting under the old woman's girth, TBN huffs, "You have osteoporosis, Helen! You can't go catching your friends!"

"Whoo-wee! That was fun," small brim red hat lady says. "Told ya she'd make it over in time."

"Yeah, yeah. You win again, Elise."

TBN rights the woman. "What would you have done if I hadn't been here?"

"That's why it's called a trust fall, isn't it? The only way to know if someone will catch you is if you fall."

TBN shakes her head as the pair sits back down and resumes giggling. TBN rubs at her back and lumbers past their table again. The cafeteria fills with noise and movement as residents recant what happened and settle back in front of their trays.

"Gah!" Lilith groans. "Now what!"

She glances toward the lunch line, where Rex is silhouetted, jumping up and down and pointing right at them. *What?* Lilith mouths, shrugging. They tried; it hadn't worked. Why does she think she can go ahead and yell at them from across the room like this?

Now Rex is grabbing fistfuls of hair and, though Lilith can't hear it, she knows Rex is groaning. Maybe even cursing. Her face is bright red. Rex jabs out her pointer finger again and finally Lilith realizes Rex isn't pointing at them. She's pointing *behind* them.

The table with Opal is empty. TBN is gone.

And so is the bracelet.

11:28 a.m.

JASON "The Nobody"

Jason and Wes don't speak as they head back toward the cafeteria. *C'mon*, Jason commands himself. *Say something. Say* anything. But, as usual, the words clog up in his throat. His fingers flex in his pocket, imagining how he'd sketch Hubert's face. The clear eyes framed by deep circles. The mouth set. How would he sketch Wes? He glances at the other boy. Wes, beside him, seems dazed. He keeps looking back down the hall where Hubert had been. Jason would draw Wes's hands first. The way they're balled into fists at his sides.

"It's, uh, it's—"

But Jason is spared from finishing the lie (*going to be okay* or *just his time, I guess*) when the cafeteria doors swing open so fast he and Wes have to jump back. An arm in teddy bear scrubs holds open the door. Quickly, Wes and Jason meld against the wall behind it. TBN steps out into the hallway, hoisting the door ajar with her hip as Opal slowly pushes a walker forward.

"I hope you weren't up to no good," TBN says to the little old woman, who swats at the air with a curled hand. TBN sighs. "Let's go on back to your room. I'm sure Mike will be stopping by before too long to check on you. Why the two of us keep bothering, I don't know. Really should just let you get what you deserve."

Jason holds his breath as the two cross to the other side of the hall and press the button for the elevator and disappear behind the closing door.

Under his breath, Wes mutters, "Wow. She really is awful."

Jason nods.

"You and that Ally girl, you're not big on conversation, are you?" Wes says.

Jason shrugs.

"Right. Let's take the stairs, beat TBN to the second floor, and trail her back to Opal's room," Wes says.

"Hold up!" shouts a familiar voice. Lilith stands in front of them, her arms crossed and foot tapping. Just behind her, Ally flashes a quick smile. She's tossing the hacky sack back and forth in her hands. "Don't you think what we do next should be decided by our *leader*? *Moi*."

Wes shakes his head. His chest rises and falls with a full-body sigh. "Fine, most glorious *leader*. What should we do next?"

Lilith smiles, the light glinting off her perfect white teeth. "Let's take the stairs, beat TBN to the second floor, and trail her back to Opal's room."

Wes rolls his eyes. "Is Rex coming?" he asks as Lilith takes the lead in heading toward the stairway.

"No," she says. "Someone has to handle clearing the cafeteria."

"Oh," Wes says, and stops. "I'll go help her."

"No way!" Lilith grabs his arm and yanks him forward. "We're going to need someone with your skill set, I think."

"Skill set?" Wes echoes.

Lilith sighs and drops his arm. Arching an eyebrow, she says, "Do you really think either one of them"—she jerks a thumb between Jason and Ally—"is going to be able to sweet-talk the way out of a situation?"

"Um, we're right here," Jason points out.

"Yeah," Wes agrees. "I guess you're right." He falls into line behind Lilith.

Even taking the stairs two at a time, the four students couldn't beat the elevator.

Tumbling into the hall, they spot TBN walking just behind Opal as she eases toward her room with shuffling steps. TBN is whispering the whole time. Jason quickens his steps, trying to hear what she's saying to the old woman without the nurse noticing them.

But all four seem to have the same idea. Lilith scurries forward, her face fierce. Jason can practically hear her expression. It's all *I am the leader!* Ally is on the balls of her feet, so she's not making any noise, but Wes clearly has no idea how to be in the background. He plods forward and bumps into Lilith, who falls sideways into Jason. Ally jumps out of the way, and Jason lands with a thud on his hip.

"Watch it!" yelps TBN, whipping around to see the trio of students standing just behind her and Jason sprawled out on the linoleum floor. Funny, he hadn't noticed the nurse's face before. He usually notices everything—too much, his mom says—but all he had taken in of TBN was the teddy bear scrubs.

The nurse is older than he had thought, maybe in her forties. Her brown hair curls into tendrils around her face, but she must've gotten tired or ran out of time before getting to the rest of her hair. Most of it is pulled back into a low ponytail, where it hangs in a mostly straight clump like the tangled tassel of a throw blanket. Her mouth is too thin for her round face, just a bubblegum-pink streak under a too-small button nose. It is like someone rolled out a big circle of peach Play-Doh and only had enough left to make miniature facial features. That is, except for TBN's eyes. They are bulbous and brown, framed by eyelashes so caked with mascara that they look like black shark teeth. She kneels down beside Jason, grabs his elbow, and yanks him to his feet.

Next to her, Opal slowly turns in her walker.

"You realize you could've knocked over a resident?" TBN says. "You have to be careful. This is a home, not a playground!" Her big eyes narrow at the four of them. "What are you guys doing here? Aren't you supposed to be working in the cafeteria? Mitchell gave most of the cafeteria workers the afternoon off for team building since you are here."

"Yes," Lilith says, and once again steps to the front. "Mrs. Mitchell also asked us to do research for a skit we're to perform for the residents this afternoon. And we have to research for an essay about all we learn while we're here today. We've left a very capable student in charge of the cafeteria and—"

"Wait," TBN interrupts, a small smile tugging on her mouth. "You mean that spiky-haired pain in the rear? *She's* the only one in the cafeteria? Awesome." She grins. "So who are you interviewing?"

Opal pushes forward and reaches out to pat Ally's bun. Jason knows if he weren't standing just behind her, Ally would've stepped away from the woman's reach. Ally's face goes totally still—not a bit of her is moving—at Opal's touch.

"Her," Lilith says, and points to the old woman.

"Opal?" TBN shakes her head. "That should be interesting. Well, go on, then. This is her room. Interview away!" Laughing again, the nurse leaves the kids with Opal, who smiles broadly at statue-like Ally.

"Wait!" Lilith says. She nods at Wes.

"Yeah, hold up, nurse!" Wes's dimple is in full force when she turns around. "Could you help me, miss? I can't seem to find my senior."

TBN's nostrils flare for a second, giving her an almost-big enough nose. "What's his name?"

"That's the thing," Wes says with a half smile. "I can't really remember his name. He's sort of tall. Sort of old?"

TBN shakes her head again. "The residents' pictures are hanging on each door. Walk around. I'm sure you'll find him."

Lilith, who has moved to stand just behind TBN, jerks her hands in a *keep going* gesture to Wes.

He tilts his head toward TBN, again deploying the dimple. "Or maybe I could interview you?"

"Me?" TBN says, and her cheeks flare pink.

"Yeah," Wes replies. "I'm sure you've got some stories. Probably better ones than the residents."

"Stories? You better believe it, kid," TBN says. "But I don't have time for an interview."

"I could maybe trail you a little, though?" Wes asks. "Until I see the picture of my senior?"

TBN shrugs. "I guess I can't stop you." She turns to Opal. "*You* better stay out of trouble."

Jason winces at her tone of voice. She talks to Opal like she's a kid. Like it's so much work just to take care of her. Like his parents talk to him.

TBN strides away and Wes is about to follow when Lilith grabs his arm. "Don't forget," she hisses in his ear, "a locker or a storage area or some place where she could dump the stuff she steals. Keep an eye out for it, okay?"

Wes winks over his shoulder at her. "I've got this."

Lilith sighs. "If only you did," she says, and touches her heart.

Ally sharply intakes her breath. She had followed Opal into her room, but now stands in the doorway, her mouth hanging open. Without even thinking about it, Jason darts to her side in an instant. Then he, too, stands with his mouth agape.

Lilith is just behind them. She looks around Opal's room and stomps her foot. "This is *so* not fair! I'm sure Agnes's room is nothing but quilt patches."

Quiet, frail Opal's room is testimony to a life that was anything but.

A poster-sized picture, blurry from being blown up too large, shows two little girls holding hands. Jason can guess which is

Opal—the one with two braids down to her chest and missing front teeth, but the same wide smile. The other little girl has her hair piled on top of her head; her knees are caked in dirt and she isn't smiling. Instead, she's yanking on Opal's arm, pulling her toward a creek behind them. That little girl is mostly a blur.

Lilith sighs again, and Jason and Ally move toward the wall of framed newspaper articles she's looking over. All the articles feature Opal in the 1970s, when she must've been an activist. Jason and Ally pause in front of one article featuring a picture of a much younger Opal, her long brown hair tied back in a bandana, holding a megaphone in one hand and a sign proclaiming *Equal Pay for Equal Work*. Next to her is another woman, her hair pulled into a sloppy bun on top of her head—one just like Ally's—holding a different sign. This one states *Down with the Patriarchy*.

Another clipping shows Opal crossing a marathon finish line, the outlines of her arm and leg muscles sharp in the black-and-white picture. Her arms are outstretched, her head hanging back as she finishes the race. The other woman is just ahead of her, but instead of rejoicing, she's still charging ahead, leaning forward into the race as if it had just begun.

There's one by Opal's nightstand from when she was in her midforties, maybe. Her head is fallen back with laughter and she's holding a small girl on her hip. The girl's tiny mouth is open mid-scream, her big eyes welling over with tears, and her fist holding an empty ice cream cone. The melting ice cream is on the sidewalk in front of the girl. Reaching for the girl is the woman who had been in the other pictures with Opal. Her mouth is puckered in a frown, but her eyes are slanted with the effort of holding back her laughter.

Other pictures in the room are more recent. A color shot is of a more recognizable Opal, her arm around the waist of the woman. Opal is softer, rounder. The other woman is as trim and fierce as ever. While Opal is perfectly in focus, the other woman is blurred around the edges, as if she was midmovement. Only her eyes, blazing into the camera, are crisp. Her eyes are green.

Like Ally's.

Jason turns toward Ally, whose eyes flicker between the pictures of the women. He steps to the side as Opal takes his spot next to Ally. She reaches out with a curled, swollen finger and touches the picture of the fierce woman's face, just over her sloppy, puffy bun. Then she turns and bounces Ally's bun with her hand. Opal's smile stretches so wide that if he were drawing it, Jason would have to figure out how to make a mouth bright as a sun.

"She looks like me," Ally whispers.

Opal *boops* Ally's bun again, then throws back her head and laughs. She takes Ally's arm and leads her in small shuffling steps to a compact vanity table. Opal sits on the round bench and Ally, after a moment, sits on the edge of the bed just next to the table.

Opal smiles and pats her knee. She hands Ally a hairbrush.

"What am I supposed to do with this?" Ally whispers to Jason. He shrugs. Ally puts the hairbrush on the bed next to her, and Opal pats her knee again. "So, um," Ally begins. "I'm supposed to interview you, I guess."

Lilith flits around the room, picking up more pictures and sighing, opening drawers and pulling out scarves or hats, checking what's behind the closet door. All the while Opal just blinks at Ally with a wide smile.

"What are you doing?" Jason hisses to Lilith, who has one of Opal's scarves wrapped around her head and is checking out her reflection in the attached bathroom mirror.

Lilith pulls off the scarf and says in a clipped voice, "Looking for clues, of course."

"By playing dress-up?" Jason asks. It's in his usual muttering tone, but somehow with an edge.

"I am *not* playing dress-up!" Lilith snaps. "Haven't you ever heard of *method acting*? I'm getting into character. If I were Opal, where would I look? Rex said TBN stashes the loot somewhere. Maybe it's in here." Chin popped in the air, Lilith pulls back the shower curtain. Jason rolls his eyes and turns back toward Ally, who seems to be vibrating with the effort of sitting still on the edge of the bed. Her knees knock as her feet bounce up and down.

A soft knock at the door draws all of their attention, except for

Opal's, who simply continues to watch Ally. The door creaks open slightly, and it's Mike, the quiet senior paired with Jason.

"I see you have some visitors, Opal," he says just barely over a whisper. Opal doesn't react at all; she might not have even heard him. "I'll come back."

Ally jumps to her feet. "No, no. It's okay. We were just going."

"No we're not," Lilith says. She has a gray newsboy cap on her head. "I'm still"—she glances at Mike—"getting stage design ideas for our skit."

Mike chuckles. "Once upon a time, you'd never see Opal without that hat on." He moves into the room, sitting on a chair on the other side of the bed. "Her Rebecca always said it covered up too much of her pretty face, but Opal said it made her feel alive to have it."

"Her Rebecca?" Jason prompts. Opal leans forward and picks up the hairbrush, handing it to Ally again.

"Yeah," Mike says. "Her Rebecca." He gestures around the room. "From the time they were knee high to a grasshopper, they were together. Best friends, always. Couldn't be more different, but somehow made a complete set."

"How long have you known them?" Jason asks.

"Since I was ankle-high to a grasshopper." Mike laughs into his hand. "Rebecca is—was—my big sister."

"And how long have you been in love with Opal?" Lilith twirls another bright scarf around her head and angles her face for a new reflection in the mirror.

"Lilith!" Ally gasps.

But Mike laughs into his hand again.

"What? I thought it was obvious."

Ally gasps again. "That doesn't mean you—"

Mike just chuckles. "I love Opal like a sister. I'm not in love with her. I've always been in love with *them*, with what they mean—*meant*—to each other. How what they had made them both better, bolder. Rebecca, on her own, she wouldn't sit still long enough to have a conversation, let alone look someone in the eye." Mike nods toward the childhood picture of the girls, and Jason's eyes snag on those blurry edges around Rebecca's image.

"My mom always says I ruin pictures because I can't sit still." Ally stares at her lap as she speaks.

Mike nods. "Sounds about right. But when Rebecca and Opal were off on one of their adventures, Rebecca was there. One hundred percent there. Opal could, I don't know, pull her brake in a way no one else could."

Opal smiles at Mike as if just realizing he is there. Then she points to Ally, leans forward, and *boops* her bun again. Again, she laughs with her whole body.

"So Opal could slow her down," Jason says. Ally glances up at him; his cheeks are so red he can see them burning.

Mike nods. "And Rebecca could speed Opal up. Like when Opal said something wasn't right, Rebecca would say, 'So what are we going to do about it? How are we going to fix it?' She wouldn't let her coast, not ever."

No one says anything for a moment. Opal leans forward and *boops* Ally's hair.

"You being here? It's the first time I've seen her smile in a long time." Mike says. "We watch out for her, me and Christi, I mean. That's my daughter. She works here. We watch out for her, but she's just not the same since Rebecca passed. A force of nature like my sister? She leaves behind a pretty powerful emptiness."

"What happened?" Ally asks.

"Heart attack," Mike says. "Happened quickly, of course. Not like Rebecca to waste anyone's time. No symptoms at all. They were getting a gift for Christi, you know, for graduating nursing college. Rebecca dropped over in the middle of the jewelry store and was gone. Opal, she already was on the decline, passing in bits and pieces. A stroke made walking tough on her. Another took her ability to talk. The doc thinks maybe another smaller one took some of her memory, or maybe it's just the getting older that makes her seem stuck sometimes. She appears to be all right, but has had some peculiar habits we've got to keep our eye on."

"Like what?" Jason asks. He sits beside Ally on the bed, the mattress bending under his weight so his hip is right against hers, and she isn't able to bounce her feet anymore.

Mike's mouth twists and he turns away. "I don't want to get into that." He rubs at the back of his neck. Mike clears his throat. "She just seems stuck sometimes. Stuck on that last moment."

Opal doesn't appear to understand what they're saying as she sits, smiling at Ally.

Mike slaps his knees and stands. "This is the most I've spoken out loud in a long time. Opal's kind of my best friend now and she doesn't talk so much . . ." He pats Opal's shoulder as he passes her. "So, ah, I hope that helped. With, you know, your interview and things." He nods at each of them.

"Be good now," he whispers to the old woman, who shoos him away with her hand.

Just as he leaves, Agnes's face pops in the doorway. "I heard from a little mouse that you were looking for your partners to do some interviews!" she says in a super bright voice. "There you are, Lily!"

Lilith spins so her back is to Agnes and only Ally and Jason can see it. Her face twists into a grimace and she locks her jaw so tight a vein pops out in a straight line down her forehead. "It's Lil*ith*," she says in the same cheery voice, even though her face is still twisted. She raises a hand and runs it down her face, leaving behind only smoothness and a smile when she turns back to Agnes's eager gaze. "And I'll look for you in a little bit for an interview. Can't wait!"

"What an actress!" Jason whispers, and Ally chokes on a laugh.

"My room is just across the hall," Agnes says to Lilith. "We could go now and I could show you my *whole* button collection before I take my afternoon nap."

"Button collection!" Lilith echoes, and that vein pops out again. "Wow. That does sound interesting." Under her breath, she mutters, "*Just* as interesting as the life Opal led as a lesbian activist in the oppressive nineteen seventies. Buttons! My word."

Lilith pulls Opal's scarf off her head and shoves it back in a drawer. "But, silly me! I promised Wes I'd help him with his interviews before nap time. I'll catch up with you soon."

Agnes claps her hands together. "Oh, yes, my favorite button is so special, I keep it right next to my—"

"Yes," Lilith interrupts, sweeping from the room with a backward wave to Ally and Jason, "tell me later, okay!"

"—Academy Award," Agnes finishes. She turns to Jason and Ally. "Would you like to see my buttons? I have one from every robot I've ever programmed."

Jason slowly pushes himself up to his feet. "I'd love to see your buttons, Agnes." To Ally, he adds, "Maybe you could spend some time with Opal?"

Ally grabs at his arm, but Jason's slips right through.

He glances back into the room at Opal and Ally. The girl's

whole body is bouncing, like it wants to move as fast as it can in every way all at once. She reaches in her pocket and pulls out the hacky sack. Jason guesses tossing it back and forth from foot to foot, even while sitting down, helps her slow her mind a little.

Opal grabs the hairbrush again. She holds it up for Ally to see. It's old, but there isn't any hair in the brush. Slowly, the old woman grabs Ally's arm. Without any pressure, she runs the brush from Ally's forearm to hand. Its bristles look soft but Ally jerks her arm out of the woman's reach. Opal pauses, smiles, and points toward a picture of Rebecca.

Agnes pats Jason on the arm. "Come on over, love, when you're ready." She winks at him. Jason glances toward Agnes's open room and back at Opal and Ally.

"Did you do this for her? When her skin got . . ." Ally shudders, shaking out her hands. "Itchy like mine. Itchy from the inside, I mean."

Opal reaches for Ally's arm again and gently runs the brush from forearm to hand.

Ally glances at the doorway and sees Jason. He ducks his head so his bangs hang over his face, wondering if she's going to be mad that he's still there, watching them. But something sort of like a smile ghosts across her face. When she speaks, she looks toward him a few times. "It feels a lot like this time when I was small—maybe five or six. My mom . . ." She swallows. "My mom was still around. She was on the phone. It must've been an important work call because she was in the back bedroom. Before Wi-Fi, her cell only got reception there." That ghost smile flickered again. "She usually paced in circles around the house when she was on the phone but she couldn't there." Ally's shoulders rise and fall. Now she's not looking at either of them, Jason or Opal. "I remember thinking, and this is dumb, but I remember thinking that I had her. For however long the call was going to be, I had her."

A soft noise trickles from Opal. She leans forward and squeezes Ally's knee, then keeps stroking with the brush.

"I sat next to her. She did this"—Ally nods toward the brush—"but to my hair with her fingertips. I think to get rid of the knots, at first. But then maybe just because she couldn't pace around. It made . . . It made me . . ."

"There," Opal murmurs, the first word she had uttered. She pats Ally's knee again.

Jason turns toward Agnes's room, just catching the whisper Ally utters in the quiet of the old woman's room. "Do you miss her?"

Jason pauses. Maybe Opal didn't hear her. But when he turns back, for the first time since he met her, Opal isn't smiling. She nods.

Ally bites her lip. "I miss my mom, too."

Opal squeezes Ally's hand. Her forehead is peaked and eyes

watery. Ally shakes her head. "No, no, she isn't dead." Ally winces at the word. "She's just gone a lot. Most of the time, really. I see her every couple of weeks. She's an important sales person." She shakes her head. "Truth is, I don't really know what my mom does. Sometimes she makes it to my meets."

She's going to run, Jason realizes. Ally pulls her arm out of Opal's grasp. "Thanks for the . . . um, time. I've got to go." Ally pushes herself up from the bed.

When she gets to the door, Opal makes a squeaking sound. She pats the bed again. On her lap she has a photo album.

Ally glances at Jason then back to Opal. Then she slowly turns back to the old woman.

11:40 a.m.

WES "The Flirt"

Wes rushes to keep up with TBN as she moves from room to room. At first, he thinks she's just trying to ditch him. Then he realizes this is how she moves—how she has to move, really. Every few steps, residents ask her for help. ("Where's my medication? I'm supposed to have it at eleven thirty and it's eleven forty-one. If my daughter knew how I was treated here . . ."; "Listen, now, I think Eloise is sneaking around my side of the room at night. I can't prove it, but I have suspicions"; "When is my son visiting me next? I think he's supposed to be here.") TBN answers each question without pausing to think. ("You're not due to have that medication until one o'clock and you know that"; "It's her room, too. That's why you're called roommates"; "He's on a cruise this week, remember? He called you from the ship on Tuesday.") All the while, she also checks charts, helps a resident to the bathroom, and wheels another resident to a doctor's appointment on the fourth floor.

"Wow," says Wes, rushing to keep by TBN's side as she marches down the hall while checking things off using her iPad. "How do you remember all of these things? Like, you know everything about all of these people."

"It's my job," TBN says.

"But . . ." Wes pauses. He's supposed to be buttering her up, getting TBN to trust him enough to let her guard down. Would what he's about to ask do that? *Probably not going to help.* In the back of his head, he hears Lilith's "skill set" comment and lets his voice trail off.

"What?" she prompts.

And suddenly Wes is blurting out what's probably the worst possible thing he could say: "No one likes you."

She snorts and goes back to her iPad.

"I mean it," Wes says. "I've watched you help, like, six people in the past ten minutes. And not one said 'thank you' or 'please' or anything. It's like they're mad at you before you even open your mouth to say a word."

Now TBN lowers the iPad, letting it fall against her leg. She arches an eyebrow. "Do you have parents, Wes?"

"Yes," he draws out. "Two of them."

Her little mouth twitches. "When was the last time you thanked them for, I don't know, making sure you have toothpaste? Or for reminding you to do your homework or to clean your room or to wait for the thing you're most excited for?"

Wes's mouth opens and closes.

"That's what I thought." TBN picks up the iPad again and gives it her attention. "I'm not here to be their friend. I'm here to take care of them. And I do a darn good job."

Wes swallows, a pit in his stomach growing. TBN isn't the villain he thought she was. She actually reminded him of . . . himself. *Remember Rex,* he orders himself. *She knows TBN is up to something.*

"What?" TBN asks.

"*What* what?"

She cocks an eyebrow. "You just nodded to yourself. What's up?"

Wes shakes his head. "I don't know. It's just . . . I'm class president."

"Of course you are."

"What's that supposed to mean?"

If TBN arched her eyebrow any higher, it'd be swallowed up by her forehead. "Well, I know what it's like to be underappreciated.

To do everything and not get any credit."

Again TBN snorts.

"What?"

"I'm sure you're appreciated, kid." TBN shakes her head. "Something tells me you're well appreciated in your school."

Wes smirks. "I guess. But it must be tough, you know, to do all of this work and not get anything back." He thinks of Hubert. "I mean, they're not even going to get better."

TBN stiffens. "So what?"

"Well, it's just . . ." *Here's your chance*, he tells himself. Here's where he can get this conversation back on track. Back to what the rest of them—Rex, especially—is counting on him to do. "You don't get anything out of it. I mean, if I were in your shoes, I'd probably, you know, want something in return. Like you might want to *take* something in return." He lets his smile stretch as slowly as melting caramel while his eyes rise to meet hers.

TBN is boiling. Her round face is a tomato, her tiny mouth is disappearing in a slash as she glares at him. *"Get something out of it?* Are you serious, kid? I'm helping them through the hardest, scariest, and most painful time of their lives. Every single day they lose more of what they once were. Every day, their ability to move, to breathe, to *think* gets a little worse. Every. Day. What I get out of it is pushing them to make the most of each second. What I get out of it is seeing them through their journey."

Wes holds up his hands, turning on his signature charm. "I'm sorry that came out wrong. I shouldn't have said that." *Something I've never said before.*

TBN takes a deep breath. Some of the red in her cheeks fades to light pink. "No, I'm sorry. It's just been a bad day. Five years ago today, my aunt died. And I didn't even know. I was mad that she wasn't at my graduation party for my master's in nursing. I never got to tell her how much I loved her and how much she meant to me. Now *her* partner is slipping away, getting worse and . . . stranger . . . every day. I'm trying so hard to make her better but—"

Wes realizes with a shudder than TBN is about to cry. *Oh, no.* He shoves his hands in his pockets and that swallowed-up feeling fills him again: respect. He respects TBN. Maybe even likes her a little. She does everything he does—keeps everyone together, even when it seems (*even when it is*) impossible. Only TBN does it without the help of good looks or a charming personality.

Wes kind of pats TBN's shoulder, not sure what to do now that he knows he can't keep trying to play her. Luckily, she shakes him off. "I don't need a hug, kid. I just need my aunt's partner to stop acting out long enough for me to let her know how much I need her." TBN straightens and shakes her shoulders like she's brushing off the emotions. "So I figure it out. I clean up her messes."

"Don't you get tired of that?" Wes asks.

"Sure." TBN shrugs. "But what's that got to do with anything?

We all have our roles to play. Stay here a second." TBN slowly opens a resident's door. Wes glances through the door frame; the room is empty. TBN steps in anyway and then closes the door behind her. But she doesn't close it all the way. It's opened just a crack, just enough for Wes to see TBN pull something from her pocket and slip it under a book on the patient's nightstand. When she comes back toward the door, Wes pretends to be checking his phone. TBN opens the door, letting just enough light in to glimmer on something shiny under the book.

"What was that about?" Wes says, hoping his voice sounds casual. "The room looked empty."

"Like I said," TBN answers. "I had something to clean up."

11:43 a.m.

JASON "The Nobody"

Jason knows one thing for certain: he will never be as interesting as Agnes.

"And that's how I taught my pet monkey to stop biting people." Agnes takes back the little photo album from where it has been resting on Jason's lap. "Want to see the scar from Mr. Fuzzbutt?" She pushes up her sleeve, but Jason shakes his head. Agnes shrugs.

"You've done so many things," Jason says.

Agnes nods. "We only get one life, I figure. Why not live it? Be as reckless and joyful and curious as possible."

"Reckless?"

Agnes smiles. "Acting without knowing what happens next. Maybe I wouldn't have so many scars, but"—she looks around the colorful room full of treasures—"I wouldn't have so many stories, either."

"Mr. Hardy said we had to be here because we made reckless choices," Jason says.

"How wonderful! A whole club of reckless story-makers! Would you like a sucker?" She plucks a lollipop from the bowl beside the bed and hands it to him. Mystery flavor.

"No, thanks," Jason says.

Agnes shrugs, unwraps the candy, and tucks it in the corner of her cheek. Jason clears his throat. "Um, did you know that mystery flavor is just a mix of all the leftover flavors from other batches?"

Agnes pulls out the sucker and studies it for a second. Then she pops it back in her mouth. "I made a quilt once. Sounds kind of like that. Take a little bit of this, a little bit of that, stitch it all together, and you have something good." She sucks on the candy, then pulls it back out, using it as a pointer to direct his attention to the patch-work quilt on her bed. "Next time, I'd probably skip that square, though."

"Is that snakeskin?" Jason runs his fingers along the leathery square.

"Copperhead. Makes a great stew." She sighs. "But they're better left alone."

"Did you get bit?"

"Heavens, no. I'm too careful for that. I just feel bad whenever I see it. It wasn't bothering me none, but I killed it anyway, just to say I had. I was thinking about my quilt and about my lunch, and I saw the snake. Thought it'd fit the bill for both. But some things can't be undone."

"It's just a snake," Jason mutters, but the words are clumsy on his tongue.

"I think the snake probably feels differently. But I'm not sure, of course. My metaphysical studies never really panned out." Agnes's head tilts to the side as she peers into the hallway. "That girl over there, talking with Opal? Is she your girlfriend?"

Jason's cheeks burn. He shakes his head and blurts out, "No!" Suddenly the words aren't stuck in his throat. Here in this little room, with this woman who has seen and done so much more than anyone ever would've guessed, his words aren't clunky and sharp. His words, for a second, are almost too slippery. "I'm not . . ." He stops himself, but new words trickle out. "I mean, I don't even know . . ."

Agnes smiles, but not the usual older-person smile after an exchange like that—the ones that teachers give with a wink when they see a boy and a girl partner for a project, or the smile with the nudge-nudge Mom or Dad might give if they saw him sketching Ally's portrait. It's just a smile. "Tough, isn't it?" says Agnes, now

River Forest Public Library
708-366-5205
www.riverforestlibrary.org

Items that you checked out

Title: Black boy joy
ID: 31865003036463
Due: Monday, August 15, 2022

Title: King and the dragonflies
ID: 31865002870177
Due: Monday, August 15, 2022

Title: Seafire
ID: 31865002761889
Due: Monday, August 15, 2022

Title: The reckless club
ID: 31865002765476
Due: Monday, August 15, 2022

Total items: 4
7/25/2022 1:00 PM
Checked out: 10
Overdue: 0
Hold requests: 2

Thank you for using the River Forest Public
Library self check!

gnawing a little on the lollipop.

"What's tough?" Jason asks.

Agnes throws a lollipop at Jason as she helps herself to another. This one's peach flavored. She throws another—grape. "Waiting for feelings to happen when they just seem to come so easy for everyone else."

Jason takes both lollipops and places them back in the bowl. His stomach is churning too much at what she's saying, at what he might say, to even think about candy.

"And then"—Agnes laughs—"there are folks who just don't know what they like, except that they don't seem to have a taste for anything."

Jason clears his throat. His head hangs forward, letting the curtain of hair hide his blazing cheeks. "They find out, though, right? I mean, at some point they figure out that they're . . . I mean, what they like. They figure it out, right?"

Agnes shrugs. "I think who—I mean, what—you love is like embarking on an adventure. You can't go until you're ready. You can try to force it. See an empty patch in a quilt and fill it with something regretful just to have it complete." Slowly Agnes unwraps another lollipop. She leans forward and presses smooth the waxy wrapper over the snakeskin patch. Then she pulls the other crumpled wrapper out of her pocket. She spreads that one next to it and nods.

Jason shuts his eyes, thinking about all the times he's sketched Ally. He sketches her because he sees something in her; something about her makes him feel something. But what? Curiosity, maybe. He hopes it is because part of him likes her, as in *likes* her likes her. He worries he sketches her only because he's lonely and sees that in her, too. Why can't he be more like Wes? He seems to have it so easy, knowing just when to smile and what to say and how to *be*. Shame fills him, shame at not knowing what everyone else seems to have been born understanding.

"Or," Agnes continues, "you can wait." She pulls a pair of scissors out of the table drawer and clips the corners of the wrappers to fit the snakeskin patch. "You could give yourself that blank spot and not worry about it being blank. Maybe one day it'll be filled up with something easy. Something expected. And it'll feel just right. Maybe it'll be something unexpected—a lollipop wrapper stitched into the quilt of your life. And *that* will feel just right."

Agnes smiles as she grabs some tape and covers the snakeskin patch with the wrappers.

Jason nods. "Are we still talking about quilts?"

"Then again," Agnes adds as if Jason hasn't spoken, "maybe you won't. Maybe you'll find your life is warm enough and you don't need a blanket after all." Jason ducks his head, trying to sort out Agnes's words. The old woman leans forward in her chair, close enough that her breath rustles the hair hanging across Jason's face.

Snip!

"What the—"

Agnes's laugh cuts off his exclamation just as quickly as her scissors chopped off his bangs.

"I always wanted to be a hairstylist!" She claps.

"What did you do?" Jason gasps as he jumps to his feet. He rushes to the little mirror in Agnes's tiny bathroom. The scream that rips out of him makes up for years of being too quiet. *"No!"* Jason's hair hangs like it always does—straight and thick to the middle of his neck. That is, except for a blunt line across the middle of his forehead, which has been clipped neatly away.

Agnes appears behind him. She pulls the lollipop out of her mouth with a pop. "I could clean it up a little."

"Clean it up a little?" Jason shouts. "I have a mullet!"

Agnes tilts her head. "Hey, now! You're right. Back in the eighties I bought a Harley and—"

"Stop!" Jason yells. "Stop! I don't want to hear about the time you were in a biker gang!"

"Well, not a gang. A group of motor enthusiasts," she responds in the same cheery voice. She leans forward with the scissors in hand. Jason dodges her. "Let me just . . ." Agnes manages to snip another chunk of hair over his right ear.

A strangled sort of cry bubbles out of him.

"If you'd just sit still, dear!" Agnes guides Jason to sit on the closed toilet seat and then shakes out a towel around his shoulders. He realizes numbly that he's whimpering. "My first haircut!" Agnes says. "Isn't it exciting to try new things?"

A few snips and the whirl of an electric razor later and Jason's mouth flops open and closed in front of the mirror. "I have to go."

Agnes waves him away and starts sweeping up the hair in the bathroom with a handheld vacuum.

At Agnes's doorway, he pauses. Ally is saying good-bye to Opal, too. He breathes out; part of him is surprised she hasn't run away already.

Opal reaches below her mattress and cups something in her hand. She shuffles toward Ally, opening her hand and pressing something into the girl's palm. Opal closes Ally's fingers around the small object. A chain slips from her palm, and Opal tucks it back into Ally's hand, placing a finger against her mouth. *A secret.* Her mouth, lopsided where it droops to the left, slowly forms silent words that Jason can just make out. *For you.*

Ally starts to open her hand, but Opal closes it again.

Ally nods and drops the object into her pocket without looking at it. Opal smiles and closes her door as Ally exits.

In the hallway, Ally tilts her head at Jason. She rubs at her eyes. *"Jason?"*

"Yeah," Jason says, sighing. He rubs his hand across the back of his now stubbly head.

"When? How?" She reaches up to touch the longer swoop of hair going back in a crested wave from Jason's forehead to blend with the shorter hair along the sides and back of his head. There's a straight, sharp part where the longer hair begins, and while Jason's hair used to swing in front of his face, now it's gelled into position. He looks like he stepped out of a 1940s movie. "Is there a barber here?"

"No," Jason says, then smiles.

Again Ally blinks.

"It was Agnes. She always wanted to cut hair and so . . ."

"You just let her?"

"Well, not exactly."

"Wow," Ally says, then blinks at him.

"What?" Jason's face flushes.

"You look—"

But whatever Ally is going to say next is cut off as Rex barrels between them.

"Is she holding a spatula?" Jason asks.

"Let's go!" says Ally, already sprinting after Rex.

11:50 a.m.

ⅬILITH "The Drama Queen"

Be the lead.

In third grade, Lilith's parents made her go to a therapist once a week to deal with her "personality." That's how they put it: "We need help dealing with your personality."

One of the first things the therapist said was that Lilith didn't need therapy. "She needs a diversion, a way to channel her energy," he had said. He was the one who suggested she attend acting classes. *And some day,* Lilith thinks, *when I accept my first Oscar, I'm going to rub the bald head of the statuette with one hand and say it reminds me of the therapist who first told my parents that their daughter didn't need help; she needed a stage.*

Okay, so that's not exactly how therapy went. How it *honestly* went was the therapist pushed her again and again to be "authentic." Whatever that is. No one is authentic. "I'm concerned that you spend all of your efforts molding yourself into a character, so you're never focusing on *you*," the therapist had said, then added, "And it kind of annoys people when your mouth makes the words they're saying even as they're saying them. The way you are right now."

"You should work on being less predictable, then," Lilith had said.

What. A. Doofus.

How could he not realize that people behave and do what they do because of influences, whether they're their own influences or someone else's? Like right now, for instance, Lilith is scouring the halls of this retirement home, allowing her skin to muddle under the fluorescent lights, all the while missing opportunities to focus on her portfolio. And while Jason, Ally, and Wes would say they're doing it for Rex, they're really doing it to feel good about themselves. Wes is helping so he can have one more person in his fan club; Jason because he doesn't have any friends thanks to his all-emo-all-the-time approach to life; and Ally is doing it because she can't stand to be left behind—ever.

Lilith knows all of this because it's her job to know people. Everyone assumes Lilith is selfish. ("You only think of yourself, Lily," Mom says at least three times a day.) But it isn't true. Lilith's

131

never thinking of herself. She's thinking of her outward portrayal, maybe, but she's mostly thinking of everyone else. All. The. Time. And maybe wondering what it is about her that doesn't make anyone else think of her unless she forces them.

How would she portray them? First step: pinpoint their motivations. This, if Future Academy Award–winning actress Lilith is being honest, is another reason to thank the therapist. He's the one who told her everyone has a motivation to be who they are. He's the one who said she should root out others' motivations.

Once you understand a person's motivation, you can figure out how to center yourself smack dab in the middle of those motivations. And, voilà. The story is now about you.

Be authentic was the therapist's suggested mantra she should repeat to herself every day.

But Lilith made her own mantra.

Be the lead.

Yet Rex, with all of her bitterness and bad hair, steals the spotlight every time she's anywhere near the group of nobodies Lilith is stuck with today. They all turn to Rex, cater to her, want to help her.

And that means Lilith has to make sure *she* is the one most important to Rex. Lilith has to be the one to solve this mystery. Which will never happen so long as oatmeal-loving old ladies keep cornering her to show off button collections.

Lilith strides as fast as she can in her platform sandals and vintage Harper's dress. (Okay, strictly speaking, the dress isn't *actually* vintage but definitely is made to look like a Harper's and that's close enough.)

Wes and TBN couldn't have gotten too far. She'd find them, trail them, and figure out TBN's motivation. Once she discovered that, it would just be a matter of seconds before she'd find the loot and win the admiration and respect of the entire Northbrook facility and, most importantly, Rex Gallagher.

Not that, from the sound of the shouts coming from the cafeteria, Rex will appreciate it. She'll probably be too busy complaining about being left alone to handle all the residents while Lilith and the rest of the crew do all the messy work of tracking down TBN.

Mrs. Mitchell's high-pitched, "Where is everyone?" drifts into the air, so Lilith risks bodily injury to sprint away, down the next hallway. *Jackpot!* Wes and TBN are talking. Lilith pauses a moment to take in the scene. Wes is supposed to be buttering up the nurse, getting her to divulge information, but for some reason, *Wes* is the one spilling his life's story.

"I have to be the one who keeps everything together, all the time," Wes says. "I mean, even at school, everyone looks up to me, thinks I'm the one who's got to handle things. But the one time I mess up . . ."

"You don't *get* to mess up," TBN snaps back, not taking her eyes from the iPad chart in her hand. "That's the thing. Once people count on you, you're responsible forever."

"But it's not like I *wanted* to hurt her. It's not like I even *knew* what they were going to do." Lilith has to creep closer to hear Wes's voice, which has dissipated to a whisper. *Who is he talking about?*

TBN lowers the iPad. With it still in her hand, she crosses her arms and cocks an eyebrow at Wes. He just blinks back at her and somehow manages to flash the dimple even while looking sad and pathetic. TBN raises the other eyebrow and taps her foot. "You didn't know what they were going to do?"

"I swear," Wes almost whines. "I swear, I didn't know—"

This is getting juicy. Lilith holds her breath and sneaks a little closer. A tall artificial plant is right next to where TBN and Wes are talking. If she can get there and hide behind it . . . but just as Lilith is about to dart across the hall to the plant, it moves. The fake plant gets up and moves a few steps closer to the pair. Lilith spots purple pantsuited legs beneath it.

Luckily, TBN and Wes are too caught up in their little heart-to-heart to notice the roving ficus. TBN shakes her head at Wes. "Maybe you didn't know exactly what they were planning, but you knew whatever it was wasn't going to be nice. Wasn't going to be good for her—or anyone."

Wes slumps. All his charisma seems to leak through the toes of his shoes. He rubs the top of his head. Lilith realizes she's copying the pose without even trying. Humility isn't something she'd played around with much. Quickly she scurries behind the plant.

"He's mine," comes a hiss from the plant. The tiny woman seeking a prom date is huddled behind it. Lilith spots her brown eyes blinking out at her from behind the branches.

"You can have him," Lilith snaps back. "I just want to know what they're saying."

"Oh," says the woman. Her tone is sweet as honey now that she doesn't view Lilith as a threat. "That nurse is telling Travis—"

"You mean Wes," Lilith interrupts.

"*Travis*," the woman repeats. "She's saying it isn't his job to take care of everybody. That he's not the nurse; she is. She's telling him to stop now before it gets so far gone that everybody's always up in his business needing help. Before too long, he'll be ugly and alone." She shifts, making the branches rustle. "Fool. No way Travis will ever be ugly and he for sure isn't going to be alone. Not with me around."

Lilith nods. "That seems to be the case."

"It is," the woman says, and she (and the tree) slide toward the pair.

"But wait," Lilith whispers. "Did the nurse say anything about herself? About, I don't know, where she *puts* things?"

But the woman shushes her as TBN starts walking down the

hall away from them, Wes trailing her.

"How do you just stop?" Wes says. It's not his usual booming, about-to-laugh voice. This Wes is quiet. Diminished. "I mean, I want to. I'd love to be someone else for a while. *Anyone* else. But everyone turns to me all the time. Like, if I wear a jersey to school, two days later, everyone's wearing that same jersey. And if I say something is cool or have an idea, then *boom*, everyone wants to do the same thing. Even if I like a girl, suddenly she's, like, *the* girl." The tree rustles at the mention of a girl, but Wes doesn't notice. "Either I think only about myself or . . . like, everyone. Take on everything, all the time."

TBN snorts. "Wish I knew. I mean, I'm not exactly setting the standard of cool around here—or anywhere else I've worked before. But I do end up being the one keeping it running."

TBN sort of smiles. The side of her mouth jerks back half an inch and, for a second, the crease between her eyes softens. Lilith stands upright in order to practice that face, using the darkened window near the ficus plant as a mirror. *Reluctant smile* she decides to call the expression. She relaxes her features and practices again. The tiny woman reaches out and grabs Lilith by the wrist. "*Get down!*" she hisses, just as TBN and Wes turn their way, but they fail to notice her or the plant.

TBN taps out patient details on the iPad. Wes stares at the carpet. TBN takes a deep breath and says, "Listen up, kid." She lets the hand holding the iPad drop a bit to her side. With the other hand, she lifts Wes's chin so he's forced to look at her straight on. "You've got to take care of yourself, too, before you forget how. Soon, you'll be letting some kid spill out his whole life to you and you'll find yourself giving him advice you should've given yourself a decade ago."

This just got really interesting. Lilith's eyes narrow. *Is Wes on team TBN now?* Lilith is to Wes's back, so she can't tell for certain, but she imagines the smile that spreads at last across Wes's face at TBN's words. She imagines it looks a lot like what someone would do when they see a friend.

What she can't quite imagine is how quickly that face morphs into something else all together—guilt, maybe? Or horror, even?—a half second later when Rex barrels around the corner just in time to see Wes thanking TBN for her advice.

Lilith can see Rex, though. She sees Rex's whole body go statue still. Sees the blood leave her face. Then Ally bumps into Rex from behind, followed closely by . . . *Wait a second! Who is the hottie?* Lilith rubs her eyes. *The hottie is* Jason!

And then a spatula leaves Rex's hand. It twirls through the air. To Lilith, it seems to be arcing in slow motion as it zeroes in on its target.

Clunk! The spatula hits Wes squarely in the head.

(Technically, it didn't make a clunking noise. But it should've.)

11:58 a.m.

JASON "The Nobody"

A little tuna casserole sticks to the middle of Wes's forehead as the spatula bounces to the floor.

"Rex," Jason says, "you can't throw spatulas at people."

But of course Rex doesn't respond. She's standing still as if freeze-frozen, throwing arm still raised.

Ally, however, laughs.

Jason nudges her with his elbow. She presses her lips together, her cheeks puffing out as she tries to lock in another laugh. It erupts out of her anyway. "Yeah," Ally manages to huff out between laughs. "You can't throw spatulas"—pause to snort—"at people."

"This really isn't a good time to laugh," Jason whispers. He can't see Rex's face, just the back of her head. But her ears are red. Really, really red. Like if her ears were alarm bells, they'd be on nuclear level. Her hands are balled into fists so tightly her knuckles look like pure bone. If he were sketching her, Jason would put crackling waves of electricity pulsating out of and around her. Rex is about to explode. He'd heard rumors of past Rexplosions. Word had it that when Rex got angry, teachers had to take her into a special soundproof, padded room behind the teacher's lounge until she calmed down.

Ally giggling right next to Rex was *not* going to defuse this bomb.

"Are you crazy?" Wes yelps at Rex.

Rex leans forward, a bull about to charge. "I trusted you!"

Next, the elevator doors across from Wes and TBN open with a *swoosh* to reveal Mr. Hardy and Mrs. Mitchell.

And then the tree in the hallway rustles. Lilith tumbles out from behind it like a hedgehog. The ficus tree stands up on purple pantsuit legs and scurries down the hall.

"*Judith!*" Mrs. Mitchell yells, and sprints after the plant.

Mr. Hardy's head swivels from his sister chasing the tree to Wes and TBN facing off an about-to-explode Rex to the spatula on the ground to where Ally is giggling next to Jason. "What is going on here?" Mr. Hardy booms. But the doors close before he can exit the elevator. Ally sucks in her breath; she's leaning against Jason but he can't look away from the clump of tuna casserole as it slides down Wes's forehead to land with a *plop* on Wes's shoes.

And suddenly Ally's laughing again so hard she slides to the floor.

Lilith jumps up, shakes out the skirt of the *vintage* dress that exactly matched the one Jason's mom had bought at Target a week earlier, and steps forward with her head high in the air. She points to TBN and says, "Where is my family heirloom?"

"Ah, give it a rest," Wes says. "She didn't do it. She's cool."

At the same time, TBN throws back her head and groans. "What are we on? An after-school special drama?"

And then . . .

Rexplosion.

ℓILITH "The Drama Queen"

Control is everything.

Yes, Judith shoving Lilith out from behind the ficus wasn't an *ideal* way to seize control of this situation. But if Marilyn Monroe could turn stinky sewer vent steam into an iconic Hollywood glitz moment, Lilith Bhat could take the lead before Rex stole the stage.

Too late.

Rex charges toward Wes and TBN. Wes jumps in front of the nurse, his hands up to clutch Rex around the shoulders. "It's not what you think," he says.

"What I think," Rex growls as she pivots and rams her now-free shoulder into Wes's chest, "is that you're a pathetic, lying fraud."

"Hey." Wes yelps. He rubs at his chest as Rex rams forward again. "You've got this wrong. You've got this all wrong."

TBN turns, her hand in the air like she's dismissing all of them. "I have work to do."

"No!" Rex screams. "You're not getting away this time!"

"Hey, knock it off," Jason bellows, rushing toward the trio. "Everyone, just calm down!" Ally, who had been rolling on the floor laughing, pushes up to her feet.

Rex reaches over Wes's shoulder and grabs TBN's ponytail. She curls it around her fist and yanks backward, making the nurse stumble. "Where is it? What did you do with it?" Rex is feral—her eyes bulging and face pale as she clutches the nurse's hair. "Where's my locket?"

TBN's arm darts back. She grabs Rex's wrist where it has hold of her hair and twists it so hard and fast that Rex's fingers contract. But even though she's free, TBN doesn't let go; she keeps twisting Rex's wrist until she crumples to the floor.

At the same time, Wes drops to his knees beside Rex. "Stop! Stop!" he cries. He pulls back TBN's fingers from Rex's wrist, but Rex shoves him away with her free hand. And suddenly Mrs. Mitchell is barreling down the hall toward them; the elevator door opens with Mr. Hardy inside and everyone in all directions is yelling the same thing: "*Stop!*"

"Get away from me!" Rex screeches in one long word. *"Don't touch me!"*

But before anyone else can get to them, TBN lets go of Rex's wrist. She leans toward her and hisses: "I've had enough of you, little girl." TBN straightens. "I pitied you for a while, but that's over. Come after me or mine once more and I will crush you, kid. I'll make it so you can never step foot on the third floor again."

"Christi!" Mrs. Mitchell yells at the same moment Mr. Hardy yells, "Rex!" Mrs. Mitchell points to the left and tells TBN to follow her.

"Rex, this way." Mr. Hardy points down the hall to the right.

Rex springs up from where she was heaped on the floor. For a moment, she turns toward the left. But Wes wedges himself in front of her. "Stop, Rex," he pleads. "Trust me, you don't know—"

"Trust you?" Rex cries. "You're just as much a liar and a thief as that piece of trash!"

TBN whips around again. "Who are *you* calling trash?"

"Hey!" Mr. Hardy yells to TBN. "Do not speak to my student that way."

"You need to control your students," Mrs. Mitchell says to the principal.

"My students?" Mr. Hardy snaps back. "Your employee is threatening Rex!"

"Oh, come on!" Mrs. Mitchell throws back.

Jason moves forward so he is beside Rex. Ally moves to her other side.

Mrs. Mitchell stomps toward Mr. Hardy and pokes him in the chest with her finger. "I'll deal with mine. You deal with yours!" She stomps back to where TBN waits in the hall, her back to the students.

Mr. Hardy crosses his arms, turning to Rex. His voice is much softer now. "You know, I didn't have to let you participate today, but I thought it'd be good for you to spend time with friends who—"

"They're not my friends," Rex growls.

Mr. Hardy shakes his head. "Wait for me here." Then he turns to the other four. "Follow me," he says. He leads them down the hall to a conference room. The backpacks and lunch bags they had given to Mrs. Mitchell were piled on top of the long table. With a glance back at Rex, he gestures them inside. Standing in front of the door, Mr. Hardy crosses his arms and cocks an eyebrow. All softness is gone from his voice when he says, "You've been up to something. All of you. I want to know what. I want names."

Cue Lilith. "Yes, sir."

"*Lilith!*" Wes hisses. Ally groans. Lilith ignores them.

"We have been up to something," she continues.

Jason sighs out of his nose and shakes his head. Lilith squelches the need to roll her eyes.

"Okay, Ms. Bhat," Mr. Hardy says. "What have you all been doing?"

Lilith straightens. Her chin pops up. "We wanted to keep it quiet. But I guess that's not going to happen now. The truth is, sir, we've been working on our skit."

"Your what?" Mr. Hardy's jaw grinds as Rex's muffled yell filters through the closed door.

"Our *skit*," Lilith says. Her eyes go round, giving her a wounded puppy dog look. "The one you told us to write. The one Mrs. Mitchell said all the old people were excited about watching. You *are* excited about the skit, right, Mr. Hardy?"

He closes his eyes and his chest rises and falls slowly. "Yes, of course I'm excited about the skit."

"I feel, sir, that you're not being sincere."

Mr. Hardy's jaw clenches again.

"We've been prepping here in the hall, but maybe we could continue to work on it in this room? And have our lunches, too?"

"Yes, sir," Jason adds. "We're really hungry."

Lines pop out on Mr. Hardy's face as he scowls at Jason. "What happened to your hair?"

Lilith clears her throat. *When did Jason decide it's okay to speak?* "Yes, so if we could have this meeting space? And our lunches? I'm feeling dehydrated and famished."

Mr. Hardy just stares at them.

"I've seen her dehydrated, sir," Wes says. "It's gross."

Lilith glares at him. *Nothing about me is gross.*

Ally hiccups again.

Mr. Hardy's nostrils flare but he waves them toward the seats around the long conference table. Ally sits next to Jason toward the middle of the table. Lilith sits at the head. Wes sits across from Jason. Wes and Ally grab their bags and pull out packed lunches. Jason and Lilith, who've been holding on to theirs, unzip their bags and do the same.

"I'm going to be dealing with Rex for a little while. I want this door open the whole time. No more of running around through the building. Got it?"

"Yes, sir," the four of them say in unison.

12:01 p.m.

JASON "The Nobody"

"What are we supposed to do now?" Wes quietly says after Mr. Hardy leaves.

No one answers. One by one, they unpack their food. Jason's lunch is in a brown paper bag. Peanut butter and jelly with no crusts, applesauce, chips in a plastic baggie, and a juice box. Mom always removes the crusts, even though crusts have never bothered him. He would've packed his own lunch, but there it was, waiting for him on the countertop that morning. He knew why: it was a consolation prize for the fight he and Dad had the night before. She always did this—some little gesture to make up for never standing up for him. A pack of charcoal pencils on his bed after school. A trip through the Starbucks drive-thru before church. An already packed lunch. He wondered if she knew how it always made him feel like a baby, needing a kiss over a boo-boo like he did when we was a toddler.

"What's wrong?" Ally whispers.

Jason follows her gaze to his ribs and realizes he has been rubbing them while thinking about his parents. Dad had been hounding him to go out in the backyard and "throw the ball around" with him all night. Finally he had given in. His dad whooped and slapped him on the back like it'd be the greatest time ever. Like maybe *this* time Jason could actually catch the football instead of having it slip through his hands like it was buttered. "Alter your stance," Dad had called then demonstrated, squatting a little with his hands out. Jason had tossed the ball back, wincing along with Dad when it wobbled instead of sliced through the air.

"Like this," Dad had said, arcing the ball back over his shoulder before throwing.

"Like this," he had said a moment later when Jason missed the ball again.

Toss by toss, just like always, Dad's enthusiasm had leaked away. Finally, just like always, he had called out, "Are you even *trying?*"

Jason had thrown the ball back too hard after that, and Dad had returned it even harder, pelting him in the ribs and finally ending the game. "Should've had your hands up," he said as Jason held an icepack to the growing bruise.

"Nothing," Jason says as Ally pulls out plastic container after plastic container from her bag. Almonds, carrots, cheese cubes, diced-up turkey, cucumber slices, a hard-boiled egg, and finally a Gatorade.

"What?" she says.

"You're going to eat *all* of that?" asks Lilith. She has fruit snacks and a Diet Coke placed before her.

"You're only going to eat *that*?" Ally responds. "That's not even actual food." She pushes the container of almonds to Lilith. "Eat something. I'd be a jerk too if I were hungry all the time."

"I am *not* a jerk." Lilith crunches down on an almond.

Ally shrugs.

Across from them, Wes unzips his lunchbox. On top of the sandwich baggie is a note. Even upside down, Jason can read it: *Remember who you are. Xoxo, Mom.*

What did that mean? Remember who you are?

Wes sees Jason reading the note and crumples it in his fist before shoving it into his pocket. "We have to fix this," Wes says. "Rex doesn't know why TBN has all that jewelry. She's *not* stealing it, she's—"

"Covering for Opal," Jason cuts in.

"Who's Opal?" Wes asks.

Jason and Ally both start talking at once. Lilith throws up her arm. "Stop. As your leader, I demand you fill me in here. One at a time."

Ally rolls her eyes. "Okay, *leader*. Here's my theory: that old lady I'm paired with—Opal—for whatever reason, she keeps thinking she's at a jewelry store. I think it's because that's where her partner died. So she just helps herself to whatever jewelry she sees."

Wes gasps. "You know what? I think TBN is her niece. She's covering for her by putting everything back after Opal nabs it."

Jason points to him. "That's right! Mike said his daughter works here!"

Lilith sips her soda, then says, "Something doesn't make sense. Why doesn't TBN just tell Mrs. Mitchell that Opal's stealing stuff?"

Jason rubs the back of his neck. The hair feels funny now that it's so short there. To get it right, Agnes had used an electric razor she had dumped a bunch of peroxide over. ("This is how I sanitized things when I helped in triage during Woodstock.") Jason says, "Because if TBN lets Mrs. Mitchell know that Opal is losing it, she'll have to go to a different floor and TBN won't be able to take care of her anymore."

"Yeah," Lilith says. "Mrs. Mitchell told me she moves patients as soon as their symptoms change." She shrugs. "TBN needs to come clean. Opal can't go stealing family heirlooms."

"TBN has it under control," Wes says without looking up. "What we've got to figure out is how to keep her from getting fired."

"And how to give Rex this." Ally pulls the locket out of her pocket and drops it on the table.

"*That's* what we've been getting in trouble over?" Lilith groans. The locket is a little bigger than a quarter. The silver on it is tarnishing; at one point, it must've had a gemstone chip in a star-shaped spot at the top, but now it just has the divot from where the stone had been. Lilith had been expecting something precious, like the jewelry she keeps tucked away in the box on top of her dresser. She slides the locket closer and opens it with her thumbnail. Inside is a picture of a boy with a thick mop of black hair and wide brown eyes. He isn't smiling. On the other side is a little girl with the same thick hair and eyes, but she's flashing a huge grin revealing missing top front teeth.

The three crowd behind Lilith to look at the pictures. No one says anything for a long moment. Finally, Jason clears his throat. "I've never seen Rex smile like that."

"Are you sure that's even her?" asks Ally.

"Yeah," Wes says. "That's her." He closes the locket but leaves it on the table. "We've got to get it back to her."

"*Or*," Lilith says, "we could focus on what's really important here. The skit."

The others groan.

Lilith pulls out a notebook from her backpack and clicks the top of a pen. "I'm fine with taking on multiple speaking roles."

"Of course you are," Ally mutters.

Lilith continues as if Ally hasn't spoken. "Rather than *each* of us playing the role of students, I'll assume the role of *all* of us. That opens up the rest of you to take on the supporting roles."

"*And* we need to do something about TBN," says Wes as if Lilith hasn't spoken.

"Why?" Jason and Ally say together.

"She's getting in a lot of trouble. She might even get fired. All Hardy and Mitchell saw was her attacking Rex. They don't know that Rex attacked her first. It isn't right."

"I don't think there's anything we can do about that," Ally says. "But we can go down the hall to Rex. Give her the locket. I mean, obviously, it's important to her. That's something, at least."

Wes shakes his head. "No, we've got to help both of them."

"Okay," Jason says. "Then we need to split up. Ally, you get the locket to Rex. Wes, you talk to Mrs. Mitchell about TBN. Lilith and I will make sure Mr. Hardy doesn't come after either of you."

Lilith tilts her head at Jason. *New haircut and suddenly he thinks he's in charge.* "That won't work."

"Why not?" Jason asks.

"Mr. Hardy and Rex are leaving." Lilith points to the hall,

which she can see from her seat. The three of them go to the door and peer to where Rex had been stationed. They see just Mr. Hardy and Rex's heels as they disappear around the corner.

12:15 p.m.

WES "The Flirt"

"Where's he taking her?" Ally asks.

"Probably to an isolation room," Lilith says. "I saw her in one of those at school once. It's a room that's all padded and sound-proofed with a trampoline in the corner."

"No, you are making that up." Wes shakes his head.

"I'm not," Lilith says. "I'm sure it's for her own safety."

"Maybe you saw a room like that," Wes growls, "but you never saw Rex in one."

Lilith's back straightens and her lips purse. "Clearly you won't believe me."

"Just give it a break," Jason says. "Everything's dramatic

enough, don't you think? We don't need you making it even more so."

"No, I do not think it's dramatic enough," Lilith mutters, then goes back to her notebook.

"Lilith does have a point," Ally says. She swipes the necklace off the table and puts it back in her pocket. "I mean, Rex does lose it sometimes. Remember in second grade? Renn Jacobs?"

Wes smirks. "He had it coming."

Renn Jacobs was a big kid, even then. In second grade, he was twice the size of Rex, but that didn't stop her from picking up him *and* the scooter he was on and tossing them both to the side after he pushed a smaller kid off it.

"So did Toby Wao, last year," Jason adds.

"Oh, man," Wes says. "Were you there for that? I heard it was epic."

Jason nods. Back in seventh grade, half the school saw the aftermath of Toby Wao snapping Rex's bra strap while he was sitting behind her in theater class. Toby left with a bloody nose and Rex had in-school suspension for three days.

"Yeah, but what triggered the epic blowup on the first day of school? I heard it was Jimmy McVay," Lilith says. "He said he winked at Rex in the hallway on the way to lunch."

Ally shook her head. "No, Jessen Andrews said it happened after he opened his strawberry milk in the lunch line and it splattered on Rex's hair. Remember it was long then? She always had it in that braid down to her waist."

"And then there's Valerie Morelo," Lilith says. "She was just behind Rex in the cafeteria, and swears it started when the lunch lady replaced Rex's hamburger with a cold sandwich, since Rex didn't have enough money for a hot lunch."

"No." Wes crumples the note from his sandwich in his fist. "They're all lying."

"How do you know?" Ally asks.

"I was there."

Lilith tilts her head at him. "Spill. What happened?"

Wes doesn't answer, just shakes his head. He never told anyone. Never would.

Wes had been selling homecoming dance tickets at a table by the door. He saw Mr. Hardy come to the cafeteria and pull Rex aside as she left the lunch line. He saw Hardy put his hand under Rex's elbow and guide her from the room. He saw her pivot away from his grasp. He saw Mr. Hardy lean in anyway and whisper something in Rex's ear. He saw the tray shaking as her hands trembled. He saw her face as Mr. Hardy led her out of the cafeteria.

Her face was a full moon—pale and round. Her eyes had been as wild and unseeing as wisps of cloud. *Fear*, he had thought then. Not anger.

But he had been wrong.

Because a few moments later, they all heard the crash. They all heard the screaming. They all heard the pickup from walkie-talkies stationed on every teacher and cafeteria worker: *"Restraining help needed in the cafe hallway! Now! Now!"* Another bellow and a tray clattered down the hall.

Before the teachers could stop them, the entire eighth-grade class ran toward the commotion. Wes had been in the front row. And there was Rex, Mr. Hardy's arms wrapped around her waist, pinning her arms to her side, her feet kicking, nailing him again and again. She was yelling, but not really. Really it was more like grunting as she heaved herself side to side. Her jaw was so tight that veins popped out like spokes in the tent of her neck. She wasn't a girl anymore. Rex was a bear, wild and roaring and untamable. Mr. Hardy was yelling again and again for her to stop, to calm down, to be still, but Wes knew she wouldn't, knew she couldn't, knew it had nothing to do with a wink or a milk or a sandwich. Whatever triggered this was *big*.

Teachers ran in all directions toward the now feral girl who had once been Rex. The nurse had her phone to her ear. "Yes!" she had huffed as she ran, "ambulance to Northbrook Middle! Student in distress!"

The teachers monitoring the cafeteria ushered the group of students back into the room, away from the hall. Some of the kids were laughing. A couple jerks imitated Rex, their arms at their sides and faces twisted. A few looked scared, like they might cry. Jason, Wes remembers, picked up Rex's tray and carried it to the stacks by the kitchen.

And Wes? He took his seat at the dance ticket table, his ears ringing. What had Rex been screaming? It had sounded like *just*. Like if Mr. Hardy would *just* do something, she wouldn't have exploded.

After that, Rex had been out of school for two weeks. When she came back—all of her hair chopped off—she was never left alone. A teacher escorted her everywhere she went.

Just. Wes hears the word again and again in his mind now.

Flashing blue lights fill the room and the four of them rush over to the window. A police cruiser pulls up.

Jason ducks his head, then says, "You don't think . . ."

Wes sucks in his breath. *Could Mrs. Mitchell have called the police on TBN? Or on Rex?* "We have to do something." Wes walks out of the room. Ally glances at them, bounces on her toes a little, and then sneaks right behind Wes. Jason rubs the back of his head and follows suit.

"Great. So I can follow you guys and get in trouble, or stay and do all the work on this skit and the stupid essay!" Groaning, Lilith only slightly pauses before she darts down the hall after the group.

"Do you even know where you're going?" Lilith whispers. "Mr. Hardy and Rex went in the other direction!"

"I'm going to find TBN first," Wes says. "Then we'll find Rex, give her the locket, and go back to the room."

"And write the script," Lilith finishes.

"Enough with the script, okay?" Ally snaps. "No one cares about the stupid skit."

"You'll care enough about it when Mr. Hardy makes us come back here next Saturday because we didn't finish our work!" Lilith crosses her arms.

"Is he really going to do that?" asks Jason.

Lilith straightens her spine and holds her head high. "Of course, he will."

"But did he actually *say* that's what he's going to do?" Jason presses.

"He didn't have to," Lilith says. "It's implied."

"I don't think he'll—"

"I am *not* coming back here. Not ever," Ally says. "I don't care about that stupid script or anything else."

Wes glances over his shoulder. "Geez, Sports Barbie, tell us how you really feel."

"Don't call me that, *Ding*," Ally says.

They've backtracked to where the fight first happened. The four of them stop and look at the spatula still on the floor and then up at one another.

"Ready?" Jason asks, striding down the hallway toward Mrs.

159

Mitchell's office without waiting for a response. Wes is on his heels, followed by Ally. Lilith, with a sigh, falls in step behind her.

"I'm thinking about getting my hair cut," she says.

Ally raises an eyebrow at her. "Why?"

"*He* gets a haircut and all of a sudden he's the one everyone listens to." Lilith shimmies her shoulder so her hair falls behind it.

Ally smiles. "I think something more than a haircut happened to him."

"What?"

Ally shrugs. "He talked with Agnes."

Lilith huffs air from her nose. "That old bat?"

Ally shakes her head. "You know, you're pretty bad at reading people." She sprints ahead to catch up with the boys.

"What?" Lilith gasps and then hurries forward, too.

Wes nudges Jason. "How long do you think we have until Hardy checks on us?"

Jason shrugs. "Five minutes, maybe."

"Great," Wes says.

They pass through by the fish tank in the lobby. Wes takes a moment to stare at the tank, catching a glimpse of purple among the blue and yellow fish. Was it really just four hours earlier that they all had arrived? So much has happened. So much is *still* happening.

Outside of Mrs. Mitchell's office are two police officers. One of them has a notebook open and is scribbling down whatever Mrs. Mitchell is telling them.

Wes, Ally, Jason, and Lilith pause.

Don't insert yourself, Wes hears his mother say.

"We don't have to do this." Jason turns to the rest of them. "We can go back to the conference room and let the adults figure all of this out." His eyes dart to the police officers.

Ally's hand closes around the locket in her pocket. Her foot taps the ground like a heartbeat as her eyes flick to each of them, settling on Wes. Lilith and Jason turn toward him, too.

Wes steps ahead, the rest of them just behind. "Mrs. Mitchell, can we talk to you for a second?"

The police officers and Mrs. Mitchell turn toward them. The director throws her hands up in the air. "Are you kidding me? Where is my brother? Why are you *still* running around this facility unattended?"

One of the officers steps forward. "So you have unaccounted-for minors in addition to the other issue?"

"No!" Mrs. Mitchell says, her face fiery. "No, my *brother* has unaccountable minors!" She stomps her foot, sending half of her body quivering. "*I* have my top employee threatening to quit, a nonagenarian thinking she's off to prom, and an octogenarian whose sticky fingers have been stealing jewelry all over this dang-blasted home!"

161

"You can't arrest Opal," Ally blurts, pushing to the front of the group to address one of the officers. "It's not her fault. She doesn't know what she's doing!"

The officer's scribbling is frantic. "Who is Opal, and what is she stealing?"

"Just some jewelry." Mrs. Mitchell groans. "Could we just focus on the reason we called you, please?"

From inside the office, they hear TBN shout, "I returned all the jewelry!"

"Not *all* of the jewelry," Lilith calls back. "I'm still missing my family heirloom bracelet."

Mrs. Mitchell reaches into her pocket. "Would that be this, dear?" She hands Lilith the bracelet. "We spotted it under the table in the cafeteria during the *very long* cleanup we had to do after lunch. But just so you know, your heirloom bracelet is also at Walmart. Ten bangles for ten bucks." She holds up her own wrist and dangles a stack of bracelets.

"Thank you," Lilith says with a surprising amount of dignity.

Jason snorts into the back of his hand.

The officer looks up from his notebook to Mrs. Mitchell. "So you have employees aiding and abetting the thief?"

"She's not a *thief*," Ally says. "She just takes stuff that doesn't belong to her."

"And I put it back!" TBN calls out again.

The officer blinks at them, then goes back to his notebook. "Let's stick to the reason you called—"

"It wasn't assault!" Wes calls out.

The officer flips shut his notebook with a snap and stares at the ceiling for a moment. Then he presses the bridge of his nose. Finally, he looks at Mrs. Mitchell. "There was an assault?"

"No!" Wes says, now pushing past Ally to be at the front of the group. "There was *no assault*. Sir."

The officer stares at Wes for a long time until he retreats into the group.

Mrs. Mitchell waves her hands in front of her. "There was a small incident involving a staff member and a rather unhinged student."

"But it wasn't assault," the officer finishes drily.

"It was self-defense," TBN says as she leaves Mrs. Mitchell's office. She pulls the badge from around her neck, handing it and her iPad to Mrs. Mitchell.

"Where are you going?" Mrs. Mitchell snaps. "We have to discuss disciplinary actions."

"No need," TBN says. "I quit."

"You can't quit!" Mrs. Mitchell says at the same time as Wes. "Why not?"

"We need you!" Mrs. Mitchell's panicked eyes are so wide Wes can see the whites shining brightly. Her mouth flops open.

Wes turns to TBN. "You said when people count on you, you don't have a choice. You have to be there for them."

TBN shakes her head. "It was nice of you to stand up for me." She pats Wes's shoulder. "You've helped me make a realization today, kid."

Wes shakes his head. "I can't be why you give up."

"Who's giving up?" TBN raises an eyebrow. "I realized that I've been keeping everyone else around me going since I was younger than you. Even though, like you said, no one likes me."

Wes drops his head to the side and says, "Oh, come on, I didn't mean—"

TBN laughs. "No, it's all right. It's true. I mixed up being needed with being important. Maybe even with being loved. But that's stupid. I've had enough, kid. Time to let someone else take the lead."

"But what are you going to do?" Wes asks.

"Nurses can always find work," TBN says. "And I'm going spend the time I can with my aunt Opal. She's being transferred to a higher care facility tomorrow."

"But . . . but what are we supposed to do without you?" Mrs. Mitchell stammers.

TBN grins. "Figure it out." She weaves between the four students toward the door.

The officer behind them clears his throat. "We're not

addressing the assault, the unaccompanied minors, or the resident thief, so let's get back to why you called us."

Mrs. Mitchell takes a deep breath. "We have a ninety-year old resident who left the facility earlier today."

"That's why the police are here?" Wes asks.

"Yes, of course! Why else would they be here?" Mrs. Mitchell asks.

The officer stares at the ceiling and squeezes the bridge of his nose again. "Do you have any idea where she might be now?"

"Either behind a ficus or in a dress shop would be my best guess."

Jason grabs Wes's arm and pulls him toward the group. "Listen, let's get to Rex before Mrs. Mitchell gives Hardy the heads-up that we're not where we're supposed to be."

Wes nods and glances over his shoulder. *Don't insert yourself*, Wes hears again. But he never has been good at listening to that voice.

"Give me just a sec," he says, ignoring Lilith's groan.

His hands shoved deep into his pockets, he walks over to the fish tank. He glances at the black curtain hanging around the bottom of the huge tank, then squats by it. "Would you like to go to prom with me?" he says softly.

Judith slowly crawls out from behind the tank. "Why, I'd be delighted!"

Wes takes her arm and leads her over to the others. As Mrs. Mitchell rushes forward and the police officer stares at the ceiling again, Judith whispers, "You'll pick me up at seven o'clock on Saturday?"

"Wouldn't miss it." Wes kisses her cheek.

When he turns, he just about smacks into Ally. She's studying his face like she's trying to put together a puzzle.

12:53 p.m.

ALLY "The Athlete"

Jewelry was never Ally's thing.

In fifth grade, she got her ears pierced. It wasn't like she asked for them to be pierced, though. Mom just came home one day and had declared she and Ally were going shopping. "Let's have some *girl* time," she had said.

First they had gotten pedicures, which kind of hurt since the technician spent so much time scrubbing the hard skin on Ally's heels. (For more than a month, she'd limp off the soccer field, missing those callouses.)

"So," Mom had said while they were sitting in the massage chairs, her voice sugary, "who do you have a crush on?"

167

Ally had shrugged. "No one."

"Oh, come on!" Mom had squeezed her arm. "You can tell me. This is girl time!"

But there wasn't anyone Ally had a crush on. "I don't know."

Mom had pet Ally's hair then and smiled wide enough for Ally to see the silver glint of fillings in her molars.

After the pedicures, they had sat through brunch. Ally had watched her mom's fingers trail to her phone and back to the tabletop again and again and again. "It's so nice to just spend time with my girl!" she had said each time. Ally wondered whom she was trying to convince.

After that, Mom had pulled her into a cheap makeup and accessory store beside the diner. "Let's see what's trendy!" Mom had picked up flowery headbands and sunglasses with stars in the corners, ignoring when Ally shook her head and backed away. "Oh, come on! Be fun!"

At the ear piercing station, Mom had said, "Ally, look! I got my ears pierced when I was ten. You can pick out whichever of these you want!" Ally had looked at the rows of studs. Her mom's man-icured finger tapped next to a pair shaped like butterflies with sparkly pink stones making the wings.

Ally had shrugged. "Okay, I guess. Is it going to hurt?"

"Not even a little!" Mom had said. Behind her, the teenage worker cleaning something that looked a lot like a gun raised her eyebrows.

"But it's going to go through my skin," Ally had pointed out. "How is it not going to hurt?"

"Oh, sweetie!" Mom had rolled her eyes. "Your dad's always saying how tough you are. Little babies get their ears pierced. It's not a big deal."

Soon Ally was in the chair and the worker had dabbed a magic marker spot on each earlobe. Then she held the ear piercing gun to her ear and pressed.

A few seconds later, Ally, wearing one sparkly pink butterfly earring, had been sprinting down the street toward home. Away from her mom.

"Stop crying," her mom had ordered when she finally caught up with her two blocks away. Mom's face was flushed enough to radiate heat and her coffee-tainted breath was stale as it beat against Ally's tear-soaked cheeks. "You stop crying this instant. It won't be tolerated!" Her mother's face had radiated solid anger. "Do you see all of these people laughing at you because you were too weak to get your ears pierced like a little baby?"

And she was right—all around Ally, grown-ups were pointing at them and whispering. "Toughen up," Mom had whisper-yelled into her ear. "No more crying!"

That was her last girl's day with her mom.

The necklace Opal gave her is the second piece of jewelry

anyone has ever given her. It feels heavy in her pocket.

The four of them walk silently in the direction Mr. Hardy and Rex disappeared. Jason keeps glancing at Ally and smiling. *He looks so different than this morning*, Ally thinks. And like she said to Lilith, it isn't just the haircut. *He seems taller, maybe.* Somehow she finds it easy to smile back at him, even though her heart is pounding. It's easy to walk beside him, even though she usually has to be first.

"What's the plan?" Wes breaks the quiet of their footsteps. "When we figure out where Rex is, I mean."

"We wing it," Jason suggests.

Lilith claps her hands. "I love improv! Give me the necklace." She puts out her open palm for the locket.

Ally shakes her head. "I'm going to do it."

Lilith keeps her hand out. "Let's be practical. I'm the best at thinking on the spot. I'll give her the necklace."

Ally shakes her head and stops walking. Jason does, too.

Jason moves a half step toward her so their arms are brushing. "Ally's going to do it."

Lilith drops her hand to her side. "Fine. Big mistake, but fine."

"Guys!" Wes motions them all forward, putting his finger to his lips. He points to an open door. The four of them crouch outside of it when they hear Mr. Hardy speaking. It's not his usual you're-in-trouble-now tone. His voice is more like a dad reading a bedtime book to a young child.

"I know it's been hard on you, Rex, but we have base level expectations for students—"

"This isn't school."

"I realize that, but this is a school function—"

"Maybe for the rest of them, but not for me."

"Will you stop interrupting me?" Now he sounds like the regular Mr. Hardy. He clears his throat. His voice dips back into the lullaby tone. "When I allowed you to join with the rest of them, I thought it'd be an opportunity for you to connect with your peers. It's important that you don't feel like you're alone."

Rex snorts.

"You're not alone, Rex."

"Whatever."

"I can't imagine what it's been like for you this year, with your mom leaving." Something twists in Ally's stomach. She doesn't want to hear what's next any more than she wanted to see what was in the locket, but she doesn't move. "And then so suddenly losing your brother—"

There's a slamming sound, like a fist hitting a table or a wall. "I did *not* lose my brother!"

"I know he's still with you, and always will be, but you know what I mean, Rex."

Ally sucks in her breath. *Rex's brother died?*

Mr. Hardy sighs. "And I know what happens next is . . . uncertain."

"What's your point, Teach?"

Wes glances at the rest of them. He whispers, "I don't think we should be listening to this."

Ally looks down. None of them move.

"The point is, Rex, you're squandering any opportunity you have to prove yourself. Get it together!" Mr. Hardy booms.

"What opportunity?" Rex yells even louder. "What have I got? My grandma said she'd only stick around until he got better." Another slamming sound. "None of us thought he wouldn't."

"I have an idea about what we can do, Rex."

"We?" she snaps.

"Yes. We. An idea you might not think highly of at first but—"

Wes turns to the rest of them again. "Seriously, let's go," he hisses.

"What?" Rex gasps at whatever Mr. Hardy has said too low for them to hear over Wes's whisper.

Lilith shifts where she's crouched. Her metal bracelet clanks against the tile. She pulls her hand back and the bracelet tumbles from her wrist to roll down the hall with a clatter.

They hear a chair pushing back in the room, and that's their cue to scramble to their feet. Everyone, that is, aside from Ally, who stays pressed against the wall.

"Yes!" Lilith says in a too loud voice. "I think you're right, Wes! That *is* the bathroom!"

From where she's crouched, Ally sees Mr. Hardy's shadow in the doorway. "What are you doing? Was I not incredibly clear that you were to wait for me in the conference room? And *not wander in the hall*?"

"Sir," Lilith begins, "after eating, we needed to find the restroom. Jason has digestive issues." She shoots him a look. "It's disgusting."

"It was an emergency," Wes adds.

Jason, his face flaming, nods. "Emergency."

"Oh, *no*!" Lilith puts her hands to her cheeks. "It *isn't* a bathroom. It's a conference room." She looks at Jason.

After a second, Jason grabs his stomach. Lilith nudges him. He moans in a dying cat sort of way.

Wes shrugs. "Better out than in, man. Don't hold it."

"Hold it!" Mr. Hardy yells. "Definitely hold it." He grabs Jason by the elbow. "Bathrooms are this way." He points down the hall.

"Oooohhhh!" Lilith bends at the waist and calls out in pain.

"Are you okay?" Jason asks, dropping his hands.

Lilith peeks up at him just enough to roll her eyes. He grabs his own stomach again.

"It must've been lunch," she groans. "The food was in our bags all day instead of being properly refrigerated. I need a nurse!"

Mr. Hardy's shoulders rise and fall. He turns back to Rex. "I'll be back shortly. Just . . ." He shrugs. "Think about what I said, okay?"

Rex doesn't answer. She's still staring at the tabletop a second later when Ally sneaks into the room.

"Hey," Ally says.

Rex nods, still not looking up. "Why aren't you with the others?"

"I—I needed to see you." Now Rex makes eye contact with Ally.

Ally takes a deep breath. "I didn't put the pieces together until after everything already happened and Wes started talking about TBN, and Jason and I remembered what we learned about Opal, and—"

"What are you trying to say, Sports Barbie?"

"Stop calling me that!" Ally's fist closes around the locket, which is still hidden in her pocket.

"Oh, did I hurt your feelings?" Rex pops up from the chair and turns to the wall, pressing her forehead against it. For just a second—between when she popped up and when she whirled around—Ally catches a glimpse of Rex's face. Her cheeks are wet. Even so, Rex's voice remains hard. "Mess with your perfect little sense of self?"

"You don't know me," Ally whispers. Her heart's trapped in her chest. *Run, run, run*, it tells her with each beat.

Rex makes a huffing sound and wipes at her nose with her forearm, still leaning her forehead against the wall. "And you think you know me?"

Ally tilts her back at the wall next to Rex. "No." For some stupid reason, the old ladies' trust fall sneaks into her mind. "No, I don't think anyone knows us." She pulls the necklace out of her pocket and holds it out to Rex.

It takes Rex a few seconds to realize what Ally's doing. Then her hand darts toward the necklace, darts back like it might be hot, then snatches it out of Ally's open palm.

"Where did you get this?" Rex twists so her back is to the wall, too. She's not bothering to hide the tears streaming down her cheeks now.

"I was trying to tell you." Ally sinks to sit on the floor with her legs in front of her. Rex does the same, but keeps her knees bent, her arms cradled on them, and stares at the locket that's gently held between her thumb and forefinger. Ally watches as Rex runs her thumb over the missing gemstone. "Opal took it. She didn't mean to—her mind is kind of stuck in this time when she was in a jewelry store." Ally shrugs. "She gave it to me."

"You've had it this whole time?" Rex gasps.

"Since just before you and TBN fought. I didn't realize it was yours until after." She shifts a little, trying not to look at Rex as she wipes at her cheeks with the back of her hand. "TBN is Opal's niece. She was trying to help her. I don't think she meant to . . ."

"Did you open it?" Rex asks.

Ally nods.

"Did everyone see it?"

"We weren't prying," Ally says. Rex pops open the locket with her thumbnail and quickly closes it again. "Is that your brother?"

Rex nods. "August." She gasps as she says it, making the name sound more like *just*. "He . . ."

"My mom left last year," Ally blurts out. "She never talked to me or anything. Just didn't come home from a business trip a couple months ago. Her stuff's still in the closet. I know my dad talks to her on the phone sometimes." Her heart beats like crazy, like she's finishing a sprint instead of whispering on the floor. It makes her voice shaky. It makes her say almost every thought, like her heart's overflowing its filter or something. "I took her pillow. It's softer than mine."

Rex doesn't say anything. Ally continues, "I don't think my mom likes me all that much."

Rex laughs. Her head falls back against the wall.

"It's not funny," Ally says as Rex laughs even harder. "I've never said it out loud before."

Rex leans a little to the side, knocking Ally. "Well, do you like her all that much?"

Ally shakes her head. She'd never admitted that before, either.

"Sucks, doesn't it?" Rex says.

"Yeah." At least she has her dad, she thinks. He pushes her to do more, be stronger, and he can be a jerk, but she never wonders if he likes her, if he loves her. Does Rex have anyone?

"This was my mom's." Rex holds up the locket for a moment, before snapping the chain around her neck. She tucks it under her shirt. "She left it on a dresser with some change and scraps of paper before she bailed."

"How long ago?" Ally asks.

Rex shrugs. "Summer before seventh grade."

"Is that when August . . . ?"

Rex winces when Ally speaks the name. She shakes her head. "No, that was a couple months later. He was . . . he's older than me. He took care of me. I found out at school."

Ally nods. Ally remembers the sound of her roaring in the hall that day outside the cafeteria. Some kids had started calling her T. rex after that. Ally had never stopped them. Her heart hammers again, wondering what she'd do if something happened to Dad. "What happened to him?"

Rex grits her teeth, shakes her head. She tucks the locket under her shirt, against her chest. After a second, she asks, "Why are you here, Sports Barbie?"

Ally's startled out of her thoughts. "I'm giving back your locket."

"No!" She laughs again. "Why are you *here*? Like what could you have possibly done to get all-day detention? You're like, school jock or whatever."

Ally opens her mouth. Maybe she would even tell Rex.

But just as she starts to speak, the sound of the rest of the group coming down the hall stops their conversation. Lilith says, "I agree, Mr. Hardy! It is amazing that our symptoms just vanished like that. It's a miracle!"

"It's certainly something." Mr. Hardy sighs.

Mr. Hardy's mouth opens and closes a little when he walks in the room to see Ally and Rex smiling at each other. "What's going on here?"

Mrs. Mitchell's clicking steps echo down to them. "There y'all are!" she booms.

Mr. Hardy crosses his arms. "Yes, here we all are. I assume you have your residents all accounted for and under control as well."

Mrs. Mitchell's nostrils flare and she crosses her arms just like her brother's. "Yes, of course, I do." She turns to the rest of them, plasters on a smile, and slaps her thighs like she's calling to puppies. "Now, I have some exciting news! It's craft and games hour!"

The five kids groan.

1:00 p.m.

WES "The Flirt"

All the trays are gone from the cafeteria. The faint aroma of tuna and peaches is the only hint that lunch had happened. Wes glances at the big black-and-white clock hanging on the wall. It's only one o'clock. *No wonder old people want to live here,* he thinks. *If I were running out of time, I'd want to go where each hour feels like a year, too.*

The tables are now filled with clusters of people playing cards, putting together puzzles, painting on canvases, or crocheting. At one long table, the residents each have a pool noodle cut into thirds. A big foam ball is in the middle of the table. Wes recognizes the two old men who had duked it out over the ping-pong game glaring at each other from opposite sides of the table.

"Okay," Mrs. Mitchell says. She's looking a little rougher than this morning. Her hair is plastered to her shiny forehead and pink lipstick is smeared at the corners of her mouth. Her folksy drawl isn't quite as warm as it was when she first welcomed them all. "So, um, pick a table and help the seniors."

The five of them glance at each other, then rush toward the pool noodle table, taking seats in between the seniors.

"The idea is that you *each* take a table," Mrs. Mitchell snaps. "Not all take the same table!"

"You weren't clear on the instructions," Lilith points out. She holds the pool noodle like a bat.

Mike, the old man Jason had been paired with earlier, pauses by the table. Jason gets up from his seat. "You can have my chair," he says. Mike shakes his head and goes over to an empty table with a jigsaw puzzle on it. Jason pushes back from his seat and follows Mike.

"There," Lilith says.

"Yes, well"—Mrs. Mitchell throws up her hands—"whatever." She sinks into one of the armchairs lining the cafeteria.

"Okay," says an activity leader at the head of the table. "Remember our rules: keep the ball going around the table. Don't be a ball hog. No hitting anyone—I'm looking at you, Henry and Alfonso; we don't want a repeat of this morning's ping-pong fiasco." Henry shakes his fist and Alfonso cracks his knuckles. "And..."

"*Have fun,*" the seniors around the table say, but in the same singsong, slightly mocking way a classroom would say *Good morning, Mr. Hardy*. Wes snickers.

The nurse then takes the foam ball and bounces it onto the table.

The ball dribbles toward a lady who's holding her foam noodle bat with two hands. Her tongue is out and her eyes narrowed as she waits for the ball. Just before it gets to her, Alfonso leans in and whips it toward Henry.

"This is what I'm referring to—" the activity leader begins. Henry pelts the ball back at Alfonso.

"Hey!" says Lilith, who's on the other side of Henry. "You almost hit me!"

"Can't take the heat, get out of the kitchen, girl," Henry bellows.

"Ugh!" Lilith runs her hands over the length of her hair, trying to smooth it. The static electricity from the noodles makes it frizz up around her head instead.

"*Ugh,*" Alfonso mocks.

"Seriously?" Lilith snaps.

"*Seriously?*" Henry sing-songs.

Lilith slaps her noodle on the table and gets up to join an old man watching television at the back of the room. "Hey, Frank," she says.

"Becky?" the man says back.

"No, Lilith. Remember? I met you at lunch. You said I have a lovely singing voice, just like your granddaughter Becky." Lilith hums a little.

"Becky can sing real pretty, too." Frank nods. "She's coming to visit me soon."

The whole table's attention shifts when the back cafeteria doors are thrown open with a clatter. Grace stomps in with Hubert hanging back from her. She strides to the table, pushing her sleeves up as she goes. No longer does she look like a blushing newlywed.

Slowly Hubert, limping and seeming a decade older than this morning, trails her. "Come on, Gracie," he says. "It's better this way."

"Don't you think that should be *my* decision?" Grace lowers herself into Jason's vacant seat.

Hubert stands across from her. "You don't understand," he says. Wes half stands, and Hubert shakes his head at him.

Henry pops out of his seat and says, "Sit down and play, or get going, Hubert!"

Hubert glances at Grace, then takes Lilith's just-vacated seat. He picks up the noodle.

The activity leader grabs the ball. She stares at Henry and Alfonso. "Last try, gentlemen. Let's play fairly, shall we?" She gently tosses the ball back on the table. Henry sighs as it rolls toward a man who weakly knocks it away.

"Good job!" the seniors around him say. "Way to go!"

Alfonso mutters something under his breath.

The ball rolls toward a woman on Ally's right. It stops right in front of the woman, who can't seem to close her hands around the noodle. She grips it with both hands but it slides down her forearms when she tries to raise it. From the head of the table, the activity leader says, "Girl, girl?" Ally's head jerks away from the old woman's when she realizes the attendant is talking to her. "Help her out, okay?"

Ally swallows. For a moment, she pauses then reaches out like someone charged with scraping up gum from under a desk. She moves the noodle and closes the woman's hands around it so she has a better grip.

The woman smiles, licks her lips, and swings her arms. The foam ball rolls a few inches away. "You did it!" the woman on the other side of the batter says. Ally shudders.

Grace leans forward, snags the ball with two hands, and throws it as hard as she can at Hubert's face.

"Whoa!" Alfonso and Henry say at the same time.

Wes hops to his feet but doesn't move as Grace pushes back

from the table and stomps to a different station, one filled with women painting their nails. Grace grabs a cotton ball, dunks it in nail polish remover, and wipes off the polish Hubert had blown dry that morning. Hubert covers his face in his hands.

Slowly the old man rises from his seat. "Sorry about the game," he says to the others, and tosses the ball back into rotation. While the rest of the residents start playing again, Hubert limps off to an empty table.

Wes follows, but stops when Rex reaches out and grabs his wrist as he passes. "Starting to doubt true love, Ding?"

Wes smirks. "I don't give up that easy." Trotting forward, he calls to Hubert.

The old man shuffles away faster.

"Hold up! Come on, man. Hold up!" Wes hurries to Hubert's side. "What happened?"

Hubert rakes a hand down the front of his face. "I told her we couldn't be together anymore, that's what. Told her to divorce me."

Wes holds out his arm to stop Hubert in place. "Why'd you do something like that?"

Hubert shakes his head. "My first wife, she passed slow. I don't want that for Grace. She's so happy. I can't be the one who takes that happiness from her."

Wes drops his arm. "She threw that ball straight at your face. I don't know a lot about women, but I'm going to guess that happy women don't do that."

Hubert strides ahead, and Wes hurries to stay by his side.

"You've got to tell her the truth, Hubert! It should be up to her."

Hubert turns and looks straight on at Wes. "Why do you care, kid?"

Wes shoves his hands in his pockets. "Because you love each other."

Hubert glances over to the table where Grace is painting her nails. She's watching them. Hubert turns and walks out of the room.

1:07 p.m.

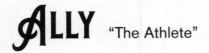 **ALLY** "The Athlete"

If you know your opponent's weakness, where they're most afraid you're going to knock, you know how to train.

If you know your opponent's weakness, you know what to exploit.

That's part of being a star athlete—getting into the other side's head space. Seeing what their triggers are and grinding your thumb into each and every one of them until they fall. Until they crumble. Until they're so distracted, so shook up, they don't even care that your pitch slammed into the glove behind them; all they want is to limp back to the dugout.

"Look for their marks," Coach had said all softball season.

"They're telling you their weakness as soon as they step up to the plate. If they stand back and then inch forward, they're scared of the ball. Throw it fast and quick. If they're staring back at you, legs hunched and ready to run, give 'em the curve ball. Scatter their nerve. Best is if they're shaking; if they need time to work their swing on the side; if they turn to the coach after each strike. Then, all you have to do is smile, and that will be enough."

But the crushing smile feels like it belongs to someone else. Like she is two people. The real Ally isn't the Ally on the mound who smirks as her team cheers her name. The Ally who sees her opponent's curled shoulders. Sees the girl's dad sitting in the bleachers with crossed arms and red cheeks at another strike. The real Ally is just there for a second, when she tastes the girl's shame like ice water against a cavity in her mouth.

"You are stone-cold, Ally girl," Coach had called when the no-hitter left the would-be batter in tears.

But the compliment is a splinter pressed into her palm. Because that time Ally hadn't been reading the opponent. At least, she hadn't thought she was. Maybe it had been just like Coach had promised at the beginning of the season. Maybe she had gotten so good at seeking out tells that she didn't even know she was doing it. Maybe she had gotten to the point where all she could see was vulnerability, even without trying, even without wanting to.

"Help her out," Rex whispers to Ally when the ball rolls to the weak old woman again. She tilts her head toward the woman, who was trying to grasp the pool noodle between arms as feeble as spaghetti. Ally shakes her head at Rex. *Do it,* Rex mouths.

Ally swallows the bile rising in her throat. She doesn't want to touch the woman again. It's not that the woman is old. It's not that she'll have to touch skin as brittle as tissue paper. It's not that Ally's scared to stretch the woman's swollen, stiff fingers. It's the blaring, overwhelming weakness of the woman—the help she needs for even the simplest task. The woman's mouth is open, tilting up at the sides. Soft sounds bubble out of her, like the babbling of a baby. She's happy, Ally realizes. She *wants* to play. She just can't.

Again Ally swallows.

"Help her," Rex says again.

But Ally can't. Her heart's jumping up in her throat. "She can't play," Ally says. "I mean, come on." She glances at the others around the table. The old woman's mouth trembles. "She can't do it."

The woman on the other side of Ally sucks in her breath. Another resident shakes his head. Even Alfonso and Henry look disgusted. Rex glares at her. "What's wrong with you?"

"Let's all take a break," the activity leader says. The residents grumble. One reaches over and pats the old woman's hand.

"You're doing just great," she says. "Just great."

Ally pushes away from the table. She turns, not sure where to go, and sees Jason and Mike watching her. She shrugs, trying to play off what just happened like it isn't a big deal. *The woman couldn't play*, she tells herself—tells Jason with her eyes. But he turns back to sorting puzzle pieces with Mike.

Ally hears someone stand from the table and knows without looking that it's Rex. Ally can practically feel anger radiating off her.

"What is your problem, Sports Barbie?"

"It's Ally. My name is Ally."

"Oh, I'm thinking of all sorts of new names for you, and any one of them would land me in another Saturday of detention." Rex's upper lip twists when she's trying to look tough. "You know, for a minute I actually thought you were cool."

Rex places her hand against her chest. Ally knows she's pressing the locket closer to her heart. And Ally knows Rex isn't nearly as tough as she wants everyone to believe. It's all an act. Unlike the endlessly revolving masks Lilith tries on, Rex found a mask that stuck. The rebel. But this close, Ally sees the cracks. *She's lonely*, Ally realizes. *She's lonely, and she thought I'd be her friend.*

Ally keeps her own face expressionless. "Why would your opinion mean anything to me at all?" Face-to-face, Rex isn't nearly as big as she seems. Face-to-face, she seems smaller, fragile even. Ally feels her cold game face set.

She whips around, right into Jason, who's now standing behind her. *How much had he heard?*

"Ally?" Jason's eyes are wrinkled at the side, the way they did when he was drawing and trying to figure out what he was going to add next.

"It's not a big deal, okay?" Ally sidesteps, looking from Jason to Rex and back. Rex's face is hard and mean. Jason looks sad. Neither has a right to look at her that way. Neither knows her, not really. It isn't like she owes them anything. "Why is everyone making this out to be a big deal? She's weak. She can't play. Why is she even in the game if she can't play?"

Jason looks at his feet while she speaks, but he's watching her from under his lashes as she steps away from them. In that moment she realizes that somehow Jason knows exactly why she has detention. He knows what she did.

"I thought you were different," Jason says. Or maybe it's Rex who says it. It doesn't matter.

That's the funny thing—but not funny as in laugh-out-loud hilarious. Funny as in sad. Funny as in pathetic. Funny as in weak.

Ally thought she was different, too. For a moment, the corner of her eyes sting. But Ally will not cry, not now or ever. She doesn't tolerate tears.

Because, really, she's just like Coach says. *Stone-cold.*

LILITH "The Drama Queen"

Being someone new is part of the fun of being an actress. While *To Kill a Mockingbird* is an all right book, Lilith admits, only one line from it really sticks with her, and it's about needing to walk around in someone else's skin if you really want to know that person. Acting is like that, but with a twist. It's being someone else in your own skin.

And usually it takes effort.

Usually it impresses people.

But this blind old man who keeps thinking Lilith is his granddaughter Becky is flat-out disappointed to discover the truth. And she isn't even trying to be like Becky. She's actually being herself.

Frank falls asleep in the middle of *Wheel of Fortune*. How he manages is a mystery since the volume is up as far as it can go.

"Frank. Hey, Frank!" Lilith nudges him.

"Becky, that you?" he asks and starts to stand.

"No, no." Lilith helps him stay seated. "It's me, Lilith."

"Oh." Frank blinks a little. "I thought you were my grand-daughter, Becky. She looks just like you."

Lilith squints at him. He's probably the whitest old man she's ever seen, down to his fluffy white hair and baby blue eyes. His arm is like a blank canvas against her darker hand. "I somehow doubt that," she says.

"Should've known better. Becky wouldn't have called me Frank. She calls me Pap."

"Right," Lilith says. "Anyway, can I change the channel? It looks like you are sleeping."

"Oh, I am just resting my eyes a spell," Frank says.

"Well, can I? Change the channel, I mean."

"Sure, Becky, you go on ahead."

"It's Lilith."

Lilith leans over the coffee table. "Frank, any chance you know where the remote is?"

He shakes his head and frowns. "I don't know that there is a remote. *Wheel of Fortune* is the only thing that ever plays on this TV."

Lilith sinks back into the couch with a sigh. What exactly is the purpose of this day? Is forced boredom even a legal means of punishment? She doesn't bother to turn around when Rex and Ally get into another whispery fight. It has to be criminal to do this to children, she thinks.

Finally, Mr. Hardy and Mrs. Mitchell come back into the room. Mr. Hardy calls out their names and motions for them to join him.

"See you later, Frank," Lilith says.

"Bye now," Frank says. "Maybe later I'll introduce you to my granddaughter. She's going to visit me real soon."

Mr. Hardy stands in front of them with his arms crossed. Next to them, Mrs. Mitchell stands with her hands held behind her back. She has a fresh layer of pink lipstick on and is back to sporting a Southern accent.

"All right, y'all!" she says. "You've had time to chitchat with our residents. Now it's time to reflect on what y'all learned!"

Mr. Hardy's jaw flexes. "Mrs. Mitchell and I have been talking about how you should spend the rest of your day. We both agree that it should be spent *quietly* reflecting. Our day here ends at four thirty." Mr. Hardy winces as Mrs. Mitchell makes the sign of the cross next to him. "So that gives you a lot of time to—"

"Write the skit!" Lilith interrupts. "Just like you asked us to."

The other four groan in unison, and Mr. Hardy nods. "That's

right," he says, "the skit, which, of course, will come *after* you write your essays about what you've learned today."

Mrs. Mitchell's bubblegum pink smile falters a moment. "Oh," she says. "The skit." She clears her throat. "Well, I'm not sure our residents will be up for that—"

Just then the door behind them opens. Agnes beams at the students, clapping her hands together. "There you are, Lily!" she squeals. "I was just talking with Opal. We *can't wait* for our special show!" She claps again and turns to Mrs. Mitchell. "When will they put on their skit?"

Mrs. Mitchell's mouth wobbles for a moment. In a shaky voice, she says, "At four o'clock, Agnes."

"Oh, yippee!" Agnes does a little skip and then points to the table behind them. "And, oh look! Jigsaw puzzles! This is such an exciting day."

Lilith shakes her head. "So sad," she mutters.

1:47 p.m.

WES "The Flirt"

Mr. Hardy leads the students back to the conference room. Lilith, of course, is first to enter the room and takes a seat at the head of the table again. Ally strides into the room and goes to the back, throwing her hacky sack against the wall, catching it, and throwing it over and over. Jason sits near the middle of the table; he has his sketchbook in front of him, his body curled over it and his pencil darting across the page.

"Come on, Rex," Mr. Hardy says. "Don't think I'm suddenly going to lower expectations after what we discussed."

"*We* didn't discuss anything," Rex says as she shuffles into the room. "*You* made a ridiculous suggestion."

Mr. Hardy sighs, his breath coming out like a leaking balloon. "Just move it along."

"I move at my own pace," she snaps.

"No," Mr. Hardy growls back, "you move at my pace when I'm in charge."

"Who says you are in charge?"

"When are you going to learn how to tell when people are trying to *help* you instead of hurting you, kid?"

"When are you going to learn to leave me alone, *Teach?*"

Principal Hardy's nostrils flare. "Both topics we can discuss Monday. In detention." He raises an eyebrow at her.

"Just one day? That's a lot to discuss."

"Tuesday, too, then."

Rex's arms are crossed and her chin popped up. Just as she opens her mouth, Wes blurts, "Stop!"

Rex's eyes shift to his. He shakes his head. Rex doesn't move, but she doesn't speak, either.

Without saying anything else, Rex slouches, her shoulder ramming into Wes as she passes by him. She grabs a chair and yanks it to a corner before forcefully sitting in it.

For a moment Wes and Mr. Hardy both stare around the room, with Lilith prattling on and on about the skit, Jason absorbed entirely in his sketch, Ally blocking them all out, and Rex partitioning herself off. *Nothing's changed*, Wes realizes. *This whole day—everything that's happened—and we're all exactly the same.*

Jason, for a while, had stepped up, been a leader even. Lilith became less obnoxious, saving all of them from getting in trouble instead of just thinking about herself. Ally dropped the better-then-everyone act and seemed to connect with Jason and Rex, too. Rex had trusted them to get her necklace back. But here they all are, back to being exactly how they were that morning—a nobody, a drama queen, an athlete, and a rebel.

Did I change? Wes asks himself. He lifts his chin, remembering. Yeah, he had stood up for TBN. He had stood up for himself. He's done solving everyone else's problems. Except that isn't even true, a little voice in his head whispers. Hadn't he put himself square in the middle of Hubert and Grace's problem? Wasn't he, even now, trying to figure out a way to keep everyone together?

"I want this door open," Mr. Hardy says. He moves a hinge on the door so it's locked in place with the door wide open. "The whole time, it's to remain open. And you're *all* going to stay inside. I can hear you from across the hall." He points to each of them. "Remember that. I can hear you."

For a full minute, no one speaks. The only sound is the steady *bam, bam, bam* of Ally's hacky sack against the wall. Finally, Lilith clears her throat. Without looking up from his sketch, Jason interrupts her, saying, "I don't think we're going to get out of this skit thing. So we should probably all fess up to why we're here. I mean, I think Hardy and Mitchell are looking for our deep over-riding lesson. And if we say what we've learned—"

Lilith clears her throat again. "*I* was going to propose some-thing. I have to figure out how to pull each of us into one character so you can take parts as residents." She turns to Rex. "Obviously, as the writer, I don't need to share *my* experience. It will come through in the writing."

"Who exactly put you in charge anyway?" Rex asks.

"Earlier, when you were off getting yelled at by Mr. Hardy, *we* decided that I will play the role of *all* of us and the rest of you will be in supporting roles. I'll try to make it so you don't even have to speak."

"How generous of you," Rex quips.

Lilith shimmies her shoulders. "You're welcome." Then she points to Jason. "You'll be one of the silent old men. I don't care which one. You'll just be lurking in the background. Should be easy enough."

"Wow," Rex mutters.

"Wes, you can be TBN," Lilith continues.

"Seriously?" Wes gasps.

"Won't be hard," Rex says, an edge to her voice. "Isn't she, like, your best friend now?"

"That's not fair," Wes says. "You don't understand—"

"Yes, she does," Ally says. "I told her TBN was just covering for

Opal. Not that she cares."

Rex swivels her chair toward Ally. "As if you're such a pillar of kindness. I saw how you treated that old lady at the game table."

Ally doesn't say anything, just throws the sack harder against the wall.

Lilith glances toward Rex. "You can play a combined role of Mrs. Mitchell and Mr. Hardy. Just be yourself—annoying and bitter—but instead of showcasing your antisocial behavioral traits, pretend to have feelings."

Ally snickers.

"And you," Lilith says to Ally, "will be one of the old women. I don't care which."

"Be Agnes," Jason says. "She's amazing."

Lilith shakes her head. "You're seriously dull. But, sure, Ally, if you want to spend the skit stitching a quilt or babbling about oatmeal, go for it."

"No," Ally says. "I can't be one of them."

"Oh, is Sports Barbie too special for that? Too strong?" Rex goads.

"Maybe." Ally shrugs. "I need a different part."

"That's impossible," Lilith says. "I'm playing all of the other parts."

"I'll do it," Jason says quietly to Lilith, but his eyes are on Rex, who is now leaning against the far wall glaring at Ally. "Ally can

199

have my part."

"An old guy? No, thank you," Ally responds. She twists her neck, making the tendons pop.

"So much for being a team player," Lilith snaps.

Ally shrugs. "I can't do it."

"But you have to," Lilith commands.

"Look," Ally blurts, "Opal—any of these residents—I don't want to be them. I don't want to even pretend to be them. They're weak and lonely, and no, thank you."

Jason leans forward a little more in his chair, like he might have to jump out of it any second. His eyes are locked on Rex whose mouth is a pinched white slash across her red fury-filled face. Her fists are curled at her sides. All her attention is on Ally.

"Come on!" Lilith says. "We're all going to be like them one day."

"Not me." Ally crosses her arms and leans back in her chair. "I'll never need someone to spoon applesauce into my mouth."

"Shut up," Rex says, but it's so low Ally doesn't seem to hear.

"I'll never be weak and drooly and pathetic. I'd rather die."

Wes believes Ally. He had been to a track meet earlier that year. It had been crazy hot out—more than ninety degrees. Ally had been the last runner in the relay race. She had been poised, ready to run, but the girl who was supposed to hand Ally the baton had tripped and it had slipped from her sweaty grip. Ally had lunged for the baton, already midstride. Her knee had hit the track, splitting the skin, but she never paused, just hopped to her feet and sprinted ahead full force, making up the time and passing everyone.

By the end, Ally's sock had been soaked with the blood streaming down her leg from a cut made much bigger by her running. After the meet, Wes had been waiting for the rest of the guys outside the locker room when Ally had come out, showered and changed. Her knee wasn't bleeding anymore, or at least it didn't seem to be from behind a big white bandage. Ally had looked around and then limped toward the parking lot. But when she saw Wes, she had straightened. Limp gone.

Yeah, Wes had to agree, Ally couldn't—wouldn't—pull off being weak.

"You stuck-up, stupid little—" Rex's feet are planted on the floor now and Wes knows that at any second, she's going to storm toward Ally.

But Jason is the one who stands. He closes his sketchbook and shoves it into his bag. Then he goes over to Ally and stands behind her. No one moves or even seems to breathe. Whatever insult Rex is about to hurl like a grenade toward Ally is swallowed down. Jason's fingers flex at his side, and then, like he's checking to see whether an iron is hot, he touches Ally's shoulder. When she doesn't move, he lets his arm rest around her shoulder. "It's okay," he whispers. "This isn't you. I mean, this doesn't *have* to be you."

Wes doesn't know what's going on. He glances at Rex, who's holding her locket in a fist against her heart. Lilith stares down at her notebook but isn't writing, just listening. A sob erupts out of Ally. At the sound, Rex pulls herself up and goes to the door. With her thumbnail, she loosens a screw from the hinge and tosses it onto the table as the door swings shut.

And Wes knows: they've all changed after all.

"You don't know why I did what I did," Ally whispers.

"It doesn't matter," Jason says. "You don't have to be like this."

"Like what?"

"Closed off. Cold." Jason squeezes her shoulder. "You don't want to be like this, do you?"

Ally shakes her head. "You don't know."

"So tell me."

Ally leans into Jason's side. Everything she's feeling, everything she's hiding, everything she's running from, bubbles up inside her and streams out of her eyes in hot tears. Her shoulders shake, but Jason's grip keeps her upright. "I'm not weak," she stammers.

And Wes is convinced that Ally falling apart in front of them is the strongest thing she's ever done.

ALLY "The Athlete"

"What's going on?" Mr. Hardy barges into the room. Rex slinks into her seat. Quickly Jason drops the arm he has around Ally and she falls back against the wall, squatting so she can bury her face into her knees. Jason sits beside her, looking at Mr. Hardy straight on.

Lilith's hand darts out and swipes the screw still on the table. Cupping it, she crosses her hands and smiles. "What do you mean, sir?"

Mr. Hardy's eyes flick around the room, starting with Rex. "Why is this door closed?"

"It doesn't stay open," Wes says.

"Of course it stays open. It's been open since I left." Mr. Hardy opens the door. It immediately swings shut. "Did one of you mess with this door? It could stay open a moment ago." Mr. Hardy stares at them through his thick eyebrows. No one moves. "Answer me!"

Rex crosses her ankles and smiles at the principal.

Mrs. Mitchell's clapping footsteps echo down the hall. "Is there a problem with your students, brother?"

"Of course not," Mr. Hardy says. He's staring at Jason, who gazes steadily back. Mr. Hardy releases the door, and it swings shut behind him.

Mr. Hardy grinds his teeth. "Okay, so, the door's broken. But that doesn't mean I won't have an eye on each of you." He opens the door, backing out the room.

Once the door slams shut, no one speaks. Rex smiles at Ally. *In what world would she and Rex Gallagher ever be friends?* Ally thinks.

Rex snorts, which sets off Ally giggling. Soon Jason joins in, too. Wes grins, his dimple in such full force that Rex has to look away. Soon he's laughing, too.

"About the skit—" Lilith starts, but is cut off by a booming chuckle coming from Jason.

Wes moves to the back of the room, where Rex is slouching in the chair pushed to the corner, near to Ally and Jason, who are laughing hysterically. Wes extends a hand toward Rex.

Mom (어흥ᅡ) ♥

1. I am thankful for mom because she is very kind + caring for example like she comforts you ~~makes you feel~~ ~~because~~ when you are hurt.

2. I like that she is a very good ~~listner~~ listener because she listens very thouroughly.

3. I like that she isn't very ~~sturn~~ and strict because she ~~doesn't~~ doesn't go crazy because you ~~touched.~~

some expensive thing,

4. I like that she is very funny and makes you feel better right away.

5. I like that she is very enjoyable and makes you taught.

6. I like that she is very smart because she teaches me on her on.

7. I like that she is very easy to communicate between she answers every question.

8.

She pauses for just a second and then grabs his arm, allowing him to help her up. Together they join Ally and Jason. Rex slumps against the wall next Jason, Wes next to Ally.

"Come on, Lilith," Jason calls. "Join us."

Lilith drops her pencil. "Fine, but you better give me decent material." And with that, they're all laughing again. Rex pats the floor next to her. Lilith delicately lowers herself beside Rex, smoothing out her dress and fluffing her hair.

Ally's smile falters a little as they each look her way. *It's going to hurt when we stop being part of this group.*

"So, why *are* you here, Ally?" Wes prods.

She rests her chin on her knees. "I'll tell you mine if you tell me yours."

Wes nods. "We'll all spill."

Lilith twists the hem of her skirt. "I don't know that we'll have time—"

"Yeah," Rex murmurs, ignoring the way Jason is watching her. "We should probably focus on the—"

"Deal." Ally holds out her hand to shake Wes's.

Without really thinking about it, Ally scoots a little closer to Jason. His arm next to hers is like an anchor, holding her skin in place so she can think about what she did and why she's there. She's still not sure she'll really be able to say it. Jason leans a little into Ally. Suddenly she's again thinking about that trust fall between the two old friends. *The only way to know if someone will catch you is to fall.* Ally spits out the words, "I filled Amelia Richard's locker with soap after the last field hockey game."

"That was you?" Lilith asks.

"You know her?" Ally's jaw clenches.

Lilith blinks at Ally. "Yeah, we met." Lilith pulls in a deep breath and stares up at the light. "Kind of hard to ignore the person sobbing in the bathroom stall behind you while you're putting your makeup on in the morning. She was there every morning the last week of school."

Ally's leg jiggles up and down.

"Yeah." Rex crosses her arms. "I know Amelia, too. Geez, Sports Barbie, why not just kick a puppy?"

"Okay, I don't know her," Wes says. "Fill me in."

Rex sighs. "So the guidance counselor comes and gets kids who need 'socialization guidance' and takes us to lunch with her once a week." Rex snorts. "Because getting plucked from the cafeteria at lunchtime is a surefire way to make the rest of you all see who to invite to your next party. Anyway, Amelia's one of the losers like me."

Jason murmurs, "That's not—"

"Save it, Picasso. Anyway, at first I thought Amelia was, like, super ironic, wearing unicorn sweatshirts and talking nonstop about sparkly vampires and angels from that series—you know, the one everyone's mom was obsessed with a few years ago?"

Wes laughs. "Yeah, I remember."

Rex continues. "But the thing is, Amelia's not ironic. She's like, more *kid* than the rest of us. Like, just a sweet kid. No cynicism or anger or . . ." She gestures vaguely at herself and then at all of them. "Her parents are like her, too."

Ally's face jerks toward Rex for a second, then dips back down to stare at her lap again. "I saw them once," Rex says, "in the guidance counselor's office. The mom smoothing her hair. The dad holding her hand. They're like, I don't know . . ."

"Pure," Lilith finishes. "I saw them picking her up once. Amelia's like that, too. Except . . ."

Rex snorts. "Yeah. Except . . ."

"Except what?" Wes says when neither of them finishes.

"She stinks," Rex says at the same time that Lilith says, "She's hygiene challenged."

"What?" Jason and Wes say at the same time.

Rex takes a deep breath. "She's not on board with the whole deodorant thing. The counselor brought it up once at our lunch. Talked about our *changing bodies* and *looking and feeling our best*. Amelia said her skin's too sensitive for deodorant. That it makes her have hives and besides, 'Mom and Dad say I'm too young to worry about all of that.'"

"She doesn't shave, either," Lilith says. "My mom and dad are super boring and dumb about stuff like that, too. Won't let me *officially* wear makeup or even shave. When she was *crying her eyes out*"—Lilith pauses to glare at Ally, who still won't look at any of them—"I offered to sneak her a razor and some deodorant. She said she's scared of cutting herself."

"I think," Rex says, "and I'm not sure I'm going to get this P.C. enough for you guys, but I think she's not entirely . . ."

Jason picks up the thought. "Her mind works a little differently?"

Rex smiles. "I like the way you put that, Picasso. Anyway, the counselor kept hounding us to *be joiners*. And, of course, Amelia's the one who listened. She tried out for field hockey and told us that she didn't need to come to our lunches anymore because she made the team."

"Everyone made the team," Ally says. Her voice is emotionless and she's still staring at her bouncing legs. "Coach didn't cut anyone. Not enough people tried out."

"So did she sit with you at lunch?" Lilith asks. "With the rest of the team?"

Ally doesn't say anything.

"Let me guess," Lilith says. "Your table was full."

Ally's shoulders rise and fall. "Yeah, okay? I sat with Stacy, Avani, Rachelle . . . the strongest players. My *friends*. How's that a bad thing?"

"You mean, Stacy, Avani, and Rachelle sat with *you*, and *you* didn't make room for Amelia," Lilith says. "*You're* the star player. *You're* the popular one. It was *your* choice."

"I'm not popular," Ally says.

All four of the others laugh.

"Sure, you're not," Wes says. "Me, either."

Ally's nostrils flare as she pulls in a deep breath. "I don't *try* to be popular. It's just because I'm the best player. It's not like anyone likes . . ."

"Likes what?" Jason prompts.

"Likes *me*," Ally barks.

"Yeah, poor popular you. The struggle." Lilith rolls her eyes. "The point is, you could've been *nice*. Or, I don't know, *not make fun of her*. But instead, the soap."

No one speaks for a second. Ally's legs are bent now, and she's jiggling them so fast her whole body seems to be vibrating.

When Ally doesn't speak, Wes asks, "Why'd you do it?"

"Because she stinks!" Ally blurts and Lilith's hands clench into fists. "I mean, not just *literally*, either. In field hockey. She missed every goal. She shouldn't have been in the game!" Ally leans back and crosses her arms. "Every game, the whole way home all my dad would do is talk about how Amelia is the weakest link. About how I had to play twice as hard to make up for her slack. How he couldn't stand to see Amelia out there, her weakness out there on display and that, since I was team captain, I had to get her up to speed or shut her down.

"Meanwhile, her parents were there every single game, just cheering for her. Holding up stupid 'Go, Amelia, go!' signs for her. Saying stupid stuff like, 'Good try!' and 'Well done' if she so much as swung the stick in the direction of the ball. I got so sick of it!"

Ally's eyes flick toward each of them. No one speaks.

"It's not like I planned it. Coach asked the parents if anyone could donate soap for the locker room. Dad got a huge box from Costco. It was in the locker room, right outside of Coach's office." Ally ducks her head, and her voice is a little muffled. "It's not like I planned it."

Lilith huffs through her nose.

"We had just finished our last game of the season. Only a few seconds left and Amelia was in a perfect position. *Perfect!* I got the ball to her. I even kept everyone else away. All she had to do was take a straight shot. I set her up! But she got the ball and just sort of batted it around, looking for the pass. The other team swooped in, nabbed it, and that was that. 'That's okay,' her mom shouted. 'Next time!' *That's okay?* I *never* hear that. Never. She messed up. But Dad was going to ream *me* out for passing to her. How is that *okay*?"

Ally takes a breath and continues. "You don't understand. Dad started in, yelling at me as I walked to the locker room." Lilith rustles and turns away from Ally, who continues, "I was tired of cleaning up after her. Cleaning up her messes. The soap was right there."

"And you could get away with it because you're the star player." Rex shakes her head. "Bet the whole team was cheering you on."

Ally forces herself to look up—to meet her eyes. She nods. Then she scrunches shut her eyes. "Yeah, they did. We were all laughing, all of us, ripping open the boxes of soap and filling Amelia's locker. She was always last to come in, since her mom and dad insisted on taking a ton of pictures of her after each game. Every single game. They probably went and thanked the coach, too, for a good season, even though it wasn't."

"Yeah, they were proud of their little *joiner*." Rex snorts.

"They think she's so perfect!" The words are jagged as they leave Ally's mouth. "They act like she's the best thing to ever happen. She's not—she barely even tries and her parents just stand there and cheer like being there is enough. They tell her, 'We just like watching you play.' Like that's all she has to do for them to . . ."

"To what?" Jason asks, his voice a whisper.

Ally shakes her head. "I wasn't thinking. I was so angry and she's always so *happy* and—"

"And you took that from her." Lilith's eyes narrow. "You were angry. She was happy. So you took that from her. It was hers, and you took it."

Ally's mouth opens like she's going to reply. Before she can,

Lilith bursts out again. "Do you have any idea how hard it is to be happy? How much *work* it takes?"

Wes interrupts. "What else?"

Ally looks away.

"What *else*?" he asks again, his voice sharp despite the casual way he leans against the wall. "I know that's not it, or the whole field hockey team would be in here with you. What else did *you* do?"

Ally closes her eyes for a second. Her chin wobbles and then she crosses her arms. "I took her clean clothes and I dumped them in the toilet. Her hairbrush, her bag, her phone. All of it. I threw it all in the toilet."

"You treated her like trash," Rex says.

"Look, I was wrong. I know it! I know it was mean. But it's not *fair*." She shakes her head as she speaks, like the words are water in her ears. "I can't get anyone to care about me—about *me* me—but they love her anyway!" Ally spits out. "They love her anyway, no matter what."

"*You're* probably the most popular kid in school," Jason says. "Who are you talking about?"

"They probably hugged her. They probably told her '*it's okay.*'"

"Who?" Jason asks again.

"*Her mom!*" Ally screams. Softer, she adds, "Her dad."

No one speaks as a shadow in the shape of Mr. Hardy pauses

by the window. After a moment, it retreats.

Lilith turns back toward Ally. "You thought it wasn't fair, so you targeted the one person on the team who knows all about life being unfair. And you sit there, and you cry, and you think it matters?"

"It was wrong," Ally whimpers. "I know it was wrong. And I'm so, so sorry."

"You were putting her in her place. Amelia dared to join one of *your* teams and you just had to show her she didn't belong. Just like people who say they can't picture me as Dorothy, that I'm *so different* than a Midwest girl like her—even though I was born in Missouri—because my *look* is *vibrant,* so—" She closes her eyes, her face crumbling for just a second. When she opens them, her face is smooth again.

Ally opens her mouth to deny it. But she meets Lilith's eyes, and they aren't glaring at her. They're wide and open and raw. Something sharp and brittle splinters from inside Ally's chest. Though goose bumps burst up her arms, Ally doesn't feel stone-cold anymore. She nods. "I was jealous of her. *I* was jealous of *Amelia Richards.*" Her arms droop at her sides. Her legs fall still to the ground. She slumps back against the wall. "I . . . I keep thinking about how she told them, how she had to look at her mom and dad and tell them . . ." She buries her face in her hands. "What did I do?" she whispers.

Jason leans back, too.

"And now we're supposed to comfort *you*?" Rex says. "Seriously?"

"Look, she feels bad about it, doesn't she?" Wes says.

"Not enough," Lilith snaps. "What are you going to do about it?"

"What can I do about it?"

"Did you call her?" Lilith asks. "Did you apologize?"

"She wouldn't want to hear from me." Ally stares at her lap again.

"Says the person who's never been targeted," Lilith snaps. "How would you know?"

"Targeted?" Ally repeats.

Lilith and Wes exchange a long look.

"Uh, I think she's trying to point out that racism is a bit of an issue in America," Rex cuts in.

"From what you hear, you mean," Wes adds softly.

Rex turns to Wes. "Yeah, from what I hear." She shakes her head. "But are you for real right now? Look at me. Look at my life." She holds up her hands. "None of you would want to be me. Not one of you."

"You don't have it that bad," Lilith says. "You exaggerate everything."

Jason's mouth pops open, but he doesn't say anything. Rex

laughs. "Sure, *I'm* the one who exaggerates, Drama Queen."

Lilith rolls her eyes. "The point is, you just naturally have an advantage."

"Maybe." Rex snorts, then turns to Wes. "Do you know where you're going to sleep next week? Know how you're going to get dinner? Have you, I don't know, said hi to your mom in the past seven months?"

She turns to Lilith. "And you—next time you're on your period, know where you're going to get some pads? How 'bout a new bag to match your *vintage* dress? Just have Mom pop over to Target, right?"

"Are you really comparing access to feminine hygiene products to institutional racism and discrimination?" Lilith sneers.

"No!" Rex yells. "No. Maybe a little. I don't know. I'm just saying we all have it rough, okay?"

Without looking at Rex, Wes adds, "Yeah, you got a bad deal. Crap parents. Not enough money. But have you thought about how much *worse* it would be for you if you were black?"

Rex doesn't say anything for a long time. "Ding, I'm just trying to get through the day. So no, I haven't spent a lot of time thinking about that."

For a minute, none of them speak. Ally feels the weight of guilt pounding against her. *You are stone-cold, Ally girl.* "How do I fix this?"

Jason leans a little more into Ally's side. "Try talking to her?"

Ally shakes her head. "What would I say?"

"Sorry, for starts," Jason says.

"No way would she forgive me," Ally whispers. Tears stream down her cheeks, but she isn't wiping them away anymore.

"Maybe not. Sometimes you can't fix something broken," Rex says, her hand holding her locket. "It stays broken."

"But you should still try," Jason whispers.

Lilith sighs. "Either way, you've got to live with the fact that you were a jerk and try to stop being so much of jerk in the future."

Ally swallows. "I guess I'll see her at school on Monday."

Lilith sighs again. "Nope. Her parents are homeschooling now."

"For real?" Wes sits next to Lilith but faces Ally. "I can't believe you didn't call her or apologize or anything."

Jason looks up at Wes. "Did you?"

"What are you talking about?" Rex asks.

Wes doesn't answer. He looks at Ally. Most of her face is covered in her shaking hands, but he can see her lips trembling. Her cheeks hollow and fill with gasping breaths. *Shame.* It's a face full of shame.

It's a face he knows well.

"A deal's a deal, Ding," Rex says. "You're up."

2:32 p.m.

WES "The Flirt"

Wes shrugs. "I didn't really know what was going on. It wasn't a big deal."

Jason stares at him.

Was Jason in that class? Wes thinks as he rubs at his temples. Truth was, maybe Jason had been and Wes had never noticed. Jason was easy to overlook.

Leaning back and letting his legs spread out in front of him, Wes says, "It was the thing with Mrs. Wahlberg."

"You mean, Whaleberg?" Rex says. "I think that's what your crew was calling her at the end of the year."

"It isn't funny," Lilith says. "She's not coming back this year."

"For real?" Jason asks.

Lilith raises an eyebrow. "Would I lie?"

"Yes," the four of them say in unison.

Lilith rolls her eyes. "Well, I'm not lying about this. She found a job at a private school. It stinks; she's a great English teacher, even if she did make us read *To Kill a Mockingbird*."

"I love that book," Jason says.

"You would," Lilith counters.

Wes rubs at his temple again. "I'm sure *I'm* not why she's leaving. I mean, there was a lot going on with her this year. She was getting a divorce and . . ."

"And . . . she gained about thirty pounds," Rex finishes. Wes looks away as Rex adds, "What did you do, Wes?"

"None of you are going to believe me, but I seriously never meant to be part of what happened to her," Wes says. "I liked her. I really did."

In addition to being the eighth-grade English teacher, Mrs. Wahlberg had been the student council adviser in seventh grade, so the year before, Wes had spent every Tuesday afternoon in her classroom, hashing out details with the rest of the student council about school dance themes, fund-raisers for local charities, and theme days for the student body. When Mr. Hardy had suggested lame ideas—pajama day even though they were in middle school, as an example—Mrs. Wahlberg had run interference. "How about something new?" She had pointed to Wes, to the Beats head-phones around his neck. "How about a day where the kids can listen to music during study hall or homeroom?"

She had noticed things. That's what really had set Mrs. Wahlberg apart.

Like when Wes's parents had separated for real. "Your smile isn't as bright as it usually is," she had said that first week. "Want to talk to me about it?"

And he did. Wes had stayed after council meetings each Tuesday; he and Mrs. Wahlberg had sat in the back of the class-room at a long table she had set up with a giant jigsaw puzzle. He'd combed through the pieces for the ones that fit together while spilling everything he felt across the table. Things like how even the house smelled different now—too soft and vanilla-like—now that Dad lived in an apartment a few blocks away. And how he didn't know where to sit in church anymore, now that Dad took a different pew and Mom joined the choir. Should he sit with Dad in the back or where he had always sat up front, but alone? He told Mrs. Wahlberg about the Sunday night dinners, about how they'd all go out for Chinese food together, a family, and how it had been his idea. How even after all of these weeks, he went to each dinner thinking maybe this Sunday would be the day when his parents realized they didn't want to leave for different homes after the check came. And, in a quieter voice, he had told her about how by the end of dinner each week, he wondered if Sunday dinner should ever happen again, now that fried rice tasted like ash in his mouth.

She hadn't told him it'd be okay or that he didn't need to worry or that he was foolish for wanting his parents to be in love again. She hadn't talked at all, just found the right puzzle pieces for the right spot and nodded once in a while. The week after they had finished the first puzzle—it had been a rainbow with the words *After Every Rain* along the bottom—Wes had felt awkward about going to the meeting that day. But when he had looked in the back of the room, on the table was a still-boxed brand-new puzzle, this one just as cheesy as the last—a big flower garden with the phrase *Your Mind Is a Garden, Your Thoughts the Seeds* forming the border.

"I don't get it," he had told Mrs. Wahlberg as they pieced the new puzzle together. "Everywhere else, everyone always wants to do what I want. But not my mom and dad. I'm not bragging," he had added, even as his cheeks had flamed, "it's just the way it is."

"I know," she had said. "You're a really charismatic kid."

"But it isn't enough to keep them together," Wes had said, throwing down a piece that wouldn't snap into place.

"That's not your job," she had said. It was their last Tuesday before summer break and the puzzle wasn't close to being finished. "I worry about you, Wes. You draw people to you naturally, but it seems too important to you that they need you, depend on you."

"That's not true," Wes had said. Mrs. Wahlberg hadn't spoken all those months while he had prattled on and on, and now she was saying something so dumb. "It's not my fault that other kids follow my lead on everything."

Mrs. Wahlberg had shrugged. "But don't you use that power sometimes to get what you want? Or to get people to like you? Stacy Stammerson didn't like you putting her in charge of manning the fund-raising station at the chess tournament; she was angry about it. *Until* you told her you liked the way her blue shirt made her eyes sparkle."

Wes had shrugged. "It was a nice shirt."

Mrs. Wahlberg had laughed. "Just be cautious, Wes." Mrs. Wahlberg had then picked up the same piece he had just tossed down. She had slipped it into the right spot. "If you spend all of your time convincing other people to like you—to be like you— you're not actually being you."

"That doesn't make any sense."

Mrs. Wahlberg laughed and said maybe someday it would. "You're a sweet boy," she had added. "You feel things deeply— when you let yourself. Just be careful. Sometimes flattery is a bit like finding a puzzle piece that seems to fit but it never quite does. I'd hate to see those deep feelings turn shallow."

In eighth grade, student council had a new adviser but Wes now had Mrs. Wahlberg for English class.

"I'm working on a new puzzle," she had said at the beginning of the year.

But by then, home didn't smell wrong anymore. He was in the choir, too, so he didn't wonder where to sit at church. And he took turns having dinner with his parents on Sunday nights—sometimes he started off the week having Italian with Mom; others, he went out for barbecue with Dad. And he knew his parents wouldn't fall back in love, no matter what he did or how much he still hoped for it to happen.

Wes had thought about e-mailing Mrs. Wahlberg or lingering in her classroom after the bell rang a few times. Her *shallow* comment had gnawed at his mind. It had rattled around at inconvenient times, such as when he stopped liking the Broncos because everyone else suddenly did, too. Or when he said Lilith was just okay during the student council's sneak peek of *The Wizard of Oz*, when really, she had been amazing.

Everything was so different now.

Now it seemed so long ago that he had sat across from Mrs. Wahlberg; it felt like he had been a different person then—a little kid—when now he knew so much more. It had almost hurt to see her now.

Mrs. Wahlberg was different, too. She wasn't wearing her

wedding ring anymore. Sometimes she had dark circles under her eyes. She didn't smile or laugh as much. And she got big. Like real big. Her clothes were too tight and then, suddenly, too loose. Where the year before she had only worn tailored suits, now she wore shapeless dresses that skimmed her ankles. The same sort of thing had happened to Wes's mom, only she had gotten thinner and thinner.

Wes had almost been able to smell the pending divorce on Mrs. Wahlberg that year.

Some of the kids had started calling her Mrs. Whaleberg. Wes hadn't. But he hadn't stopped them, either.

Maybe he even would've done something—brought her a puzzle, maybe, and spread it on the now-empty table in the back—but the guys were always waiting for him after class, and her sadness brought him down.

Sitting now surrounded by the other four, Wes doesn't share any of that. He skips ahead. "Our *To Kill a Mockingbird* essays were due the day after the Spring Fling. Mrs. Wahlberg had been student council adviser the year before. She *knew* how much work it took to pull that dance off! And we had to do it on a Thursday that year, since the show," Wes looks at Lilith, "was *supposed* to be Friday night."

He sighs and continues. "Right after school until the dance, I had to help set up. Everyone needed me to okay everything

223

they did for decorations, for song choices, for lighting. For everything, everyone needed me. Then the dance didn't clear out until nine thirty, and I had to help clean up. I was there until, like, eleven! I didn't have any time to do the essay. None of us did. I told the other guys she'd give us a pass, let us turn in our papers late."

"But," Jason says, "she had the due date on the white board for, like, a month. For a week, she had said that the Thursday night dance wasn't an excuse."

"Dude, even *I* turned in the paper on time," Rex adds.

"I didn't, okay? And so the rest of the council didn't, either. The next day, I told Mrs. Wahlberg we needed an extension. She wouldn't budge."

Rex snorts.

"That's not funny," Lilith snaps.

Rex shrugs. "Sorry, but she'd be tough to budge."

"Apology not accepted." Lilith fluffs her hair and crosses her hands on her lap.

"So, what did you do?" Ally asks. It's the first time she's spoken since confessing her prank.

"My English class was after lunch. Mrs. Wahlberg always ate in the classroom. When we came in, she always closed her laptop but not before we could see that she was on Facebook. Like, every day, she was on Facebook during her lunch break."

Ally shifts. "My dad's obsessed with Facebook. He's on it all of the time."

"My parents aren't. They're too busy reading books and being boring," Lilith says.

"Anyway," Wes continues, "the guys and I sort of found her page one day. All she posted were these stupid inspirational memes about coming out on the other side of things and seeing rainbows and all that crap."

Wes glances at Jason, who's watching him, and Wes knows Jason sees right through him. Maybe even knows how much those stupid sayings meant to him when Mrs. Wahlberg was sharing them with him a year earlier. He forces out the next sticky-as-tar words: "And her profile picture? She hadn't changed that in months. I mean, in about a thirty pounds."

No one laughs, not even Rex.

"What'd you do, Wes?" Ally asks again.

"*I* didn't do it. I didn't know what the guys were planning to do, okay?"

Rex raises an eyebrow at him.

"Ashley had this idea," Wes continues, "to get back at Mrs. Wahlberg by using her Facebook page. I didn't know the details. For real, I didn't." In fact, when the guys had come to him, busting up and saying they had an idea, Wes had held up his hands and told them not to tell him—that he didn't want to know. "They just said they needed her to be distracted, for like, a couple minutes after class. Just enough time for them to grab the laptop." Wes rubs at his temples then the back of his neck. "So I brought her a gift—a jigsaw puzzle of a kitten. I told her it was, like, a sorry or whatever for the late assignment."

He swallows, remembering Mrs. Wahlberg's face. She had smiled and her eyes had filled with tears. "There's the Wes I knew," she had said, even as Wes had shifted so her back would be at the front of the room, where Ashley was nabbing the laptop. "I can't change your grade, you know."

"You sure?" Wes had asked and smiled in that way he knew usually got people to smile back.

Mrs. Wahlberg had smiled, but it was in her now-usual small, sad way. "It's a tough lesson, I know. But you and I, we're not new to tough lessons, are we?"

Wes clears his throat now, figuring out how to own up to what he had done to the others.

Lilith asks, "What did Ashley do with the laptop?"

Wes sighs again. "He changed her profile picture. Posted a few fake things."

"To what? What kind of fake things?" Rex asks.

"To a whale," Wes whispers. "He changed her profile picture to a whale. He changed her status to something about being beached and alone." Wes stares at his lap.

"What was it exactly?" Jason asks, and Wes both hates and is grateful to him for asking.

"It said, 'This lonely beached whale would be better off dead. I should just kill myself.'"

Rex sucks in her breath. She jumps to her feet. "How could you do that?" she gasps.

Wes shakes his head. His voice isn't a whisper anymore when he says, "I didn't! Remember? I didn't do it! Ashley did."

"So why isn't *he* here?" Lilith asks.

"He snuck the laptop into the teachers' lounge. No one knew who did it. All Hardy and Mrs. Wahlberg knew was that I distracted her. I was going to be expelled over it, but Ashley came forward. I *didn't* tell on him. He came forward. So I have to be here today, and he gets in-school suspension for the first month of school."

"So you let Ashley fat shame her? Let him tell her she should die? But you think we should care that you weren't the one who told on *him*. You're as disgusting as Ally," Lilith says, her eyes wide.

Ally's face flames, but she doesn't say anything.

"Come on," Jason says. "That's not—"

"No, she's right," Wes says. "Mrs. Wahlberg was—is—a good person. She didn't deserve that." He suddenly can't block out the sound of Mrs. Wahlberg crying in Mr. Hardy's office.

"No one does," says Rex, leaning against the wall.

"We've all made mistakes. We're all going to do better." Ally's eyes dart to the rest of them. "Wes and I told you what we did. It's only fair for you guys do the same."

Lilith shifts. "What I did was *nothing* like what you guys did. It was justified."

"Really?" Rex crosses her arms and stares at Lilith. "That's not what I heard."

"Oh, God." Lilith moans. "Even *you* heard about it?"

Rex smirks. "Yeah, finding out someone might have as short a fuse as me is kind of comforting."

"Yeah, I heard about this, too," Ally says. "You freaked out on the *Wizard of Oz* set?"

"You don't know the *whole* story," Lilith says primly.

Jason leans forward. "So fill us in."

2:46 p.m.

𝕷ILITH "The Drama Queen"

"It wasn't a big deal." Lilith straightens her dress in front of her. "Really, it's not even worth talking about."

The four of them groan.

"Come on," Wes says. "Just spill already." He crosses his hands behind his head. "It'll make you feel better."

"Yeah," Ally agrees. "I don't know why, but I do feel better." Lilith glares at her. "Don't get me wrong—I'm . . ."

"Ashamed? Horrified? Regretful?"

Ally snorts. "Yeah. All of those. But also? I . . . I'm going to call Amelia tonight when we get home." She nods to herself and then smiles at Lilith.

Lilith raises an eyebrow, smiling at Jason. "Okay. Your turn."

"No, no, no, no!" Wes says.

"I don't think so," Jason adds.

"Not even close." Rex laughs.

"Fine! I got angry. Really angry." Lilith pulls in a deep breath. "Look, we had been working on *The Wizard of Oz* for months. You know Mr. Ackins, the drama teacher, right?"

"Yeah," Wes says. "He's awesome. I had him for study hall. He'd let me and the guys sit in the back and talk the whole time."

"He's *not* a nice guy," Jason says.

Lilith stares at Jason for a moment. Then she nods. "He's the kind of not-nice guy who seems like a nice guy for a long time. So when Pedro put on the Cowardly Lion costume and couldn't get it to zip, he told him it was all right, that they'd figure out a way to cover the zipper. But when Pedro walked away and someone joked that Pedro could be the Cowardly Lardy instead, Mr. Ackins just laughed. Pedro didn't hear it, so I guess he thought it was all right, but he . . ."

"Isn't a nice guy," Jason finished. "He did a lot of that kind of stuff, to a lot of people."

Lilith looks down at her lap. "I thought at first that it sort of made him cool, like you didn't have to censor what you said around him. He was, like, one of us. A kid, too, you know? But then he stopped being cool. At the beginning of the year, when we first started doing theater, I was, like, *his* person. It was the first year the middle school offered drama as an elective, and his first year as a teacher, and I think he was still figuring stuff out. I . . . I felt like his assistant or something. But then—"

"You stopped being in his little club." Jason twirls his pencil through his fingers. "I noticed that about him. He had little clusters of kids he thought were cool. In study hall, it was you." Jason nods toward Wes. "I had him for social studies, and he always called on the same four kids, even though they didn't take anything seriously. But they joked around with him as if he were their buddy. Meanwhile, kids like Barry O'Neal—you know . . ."

"Nerds?" Rex says.

Jason nods. "He'd go from being all smiling and fun to one of those kids and you could just see on his face the, I don't know, frustration, maybe? His face would go hard. As if he thought it was such a drag that he had to teach those kids, too."

Wes leans forward. "Did you guys know he was a Northbrook High quarterback? There's a trophy case outside the high school gym with his name on it. I saw it when we went for that tour of the high school."

"Yeah," Lilith says. "I think he still thinks he's a super cool guy at school. Like he's still in high school instead of a middle school social studies teacher."

"He was my homeroom teacher. Me and Jason," Rex says. "I

don't know how to even say it. It was like he didn't see me. His eyes just would glide right past me." She shrugs. "The only time he ever talked to me was when the nurse was doing lice checks. It was the beginning of homeroom, after everyone had settled, and he said, 'Rex Gallagher, you made it to the nurse for a check, right?' He said it like he was being helpful, but I was the only one he asked. Everyone laughed. Not a big deal, but still."

"I didn't laugh," Jason says.

Ally snorts.

"What?" Rex says.

"It's just, whenever we say 'it's not a big deal,' it's a big deal. A really big deal. We should stop saying that."

Rex smiles. "Anyway, Lilith, keep going."

"Well, at some point during that year, I guess he realized that I'm not one of the cool kids. He stopped listening to my ideas. And he scraped all of these plans for making a bunch of little plays and decided we'd only do one: *The Wizard of Oz*.

"He made reading the book, researching the original cast, the filmography, the set design, all of it, the whole focus for the second half of the year. It wasn't until two months before school ended that we began actually rehearsing the play."

"Right," Wes says, "with the actual show supposed to happen the day after the dance."

Lilith nods. "The last day of school. From the very beginning,

I was Dorothy, of course. It was *my* role. I was the lead of production the semester before." Lilith's eyes narrow and her nostrils flare. "And then in comes Veronica Watkins. *Seven weeks* before production, she moves in, blabbing on and on about her experience—she was in a ringworm medicine commercial. Ringworm! I was the one who had studied every bit of that play. It was *my* part. *Mine.*"

Rex's eyes widen as Lilith's hands curl into fists.

Lilith takes another deep breath, letting it out super slowly. "She was jealous of me. She turned Mr. Ackins against me." Lilith brushes some imaginary dust off her shoulder. "I got angry."

"That's not exactly what happened, though, is it?" Wes says.

Lilith glares at him.

Jason leans forward. "You said you'd share the *whole* story."

Actors and directors are supposed to be in sync with each other. Directors are supposed to have darlings with whom they love to work—actors that they'll insist on casting in a starring role if they're going to take on a particular production.

Mr. Ackins could've been David O. Russell to Lilith's Jennifer Lawrence. He, along with her therapist, *could've* been the ones thanked during her first Academy Award acceptance speech (her second speech would be just to point upward and mouth *thank you,* and the third and all subsequent wins would be dedicated to furthering awareness of whichever social or environmental issue was trending). But now? She'd never, ever thank Mr. Ackins, onstage or anywhere. Ever.

Lilith had worked for weeks to nail "Over the Rainbow," practicing it and feeling it so deeply that when Dorothy asks "why, oh, why" couldn't she go over the rainbow, Lilith wasn't pretending to hold back tears. She *was* holding them back. She lived and breathed Dorothy for months, even catching herself skipping down the hall on the way to class like she was following the yellow brick road.

Two months before production—just around when the art team began setting up designs—Lilith practiced the signature song onstage. Mr. Ackins was sitting in the front row, making notes about the set design and laughing once in a while at what the student council kids (who were there to check out the set, too) behind him said. But when Lilith began belting out the song, Mr. Ackins made a phone call. *A phone call!*

At the end of rehearsal that day, Mr. Ackins thanked each and every one of the students by name, saying what they had contributed. When it came to the end, Lilith already was beaming, knowing he kept the star for last. But instead, all he added was, "And then, of course, there was Lilith." He said it like she was a big joke. Some people laughed while others applauded.

In the conference room all these months later, Lilith's heart hammers. She scrunches shut her eyes.

"I don't care if people don't like me. I mean, I'm used to people not liking me. That's okay. Mr. Ackins didn't have to like me. But he did have to *appreciate* what I did—and I was amazing as Dorothy! I was. And he didn't appreciate it. Not even a little."

"I'm sure it wasn't that bad," Wes says. "I mean, maybe he let you be Dorothy."

"Until Veronica Watkins showed up. And, honestly?" Lilith leans against the wall. "Who moves in mid-March? We had, like, seven weeks of school left! Seven weeks of middle school! Who does that?" Lilith's jaw grinds. "Veronica Watkins. That's who."

"The cute little blonde girl?" Rex's forehead wrinkles. "Twinkle Toots?"

"That's what you call her?" Jason laughs. "She does look a lot like a fairy, I guess. Like Tinker Bell."

"Yes!" Lilith shouts. "She's tiny and has a sweet little voice, and is so bouncy and bright. You know what? I don't hate her. I really don't. In fact, when I saw her, I was excited. She was a perfect Glinda."

"Glinda?" Rex asks.

"The good witch!" Lilith says. "The one who directs Dorothy" —she points to herself—"down the yellow brick road."

"Yeah," Jason says. "The part was open. Since none of the other girls in the production wanted to sing next to Lilith, we were going to have to get a guy to do the part and call him Glen the

Good Witch."

"Oh!" Lilith says. "You heard about that?"

"Yeah," Jason says. He sort of huffs. "I was around."

"Oh." Lilith's mouth puckers. "I didn't see you . . ."

"I know," Jason says.

"*Anyway,*" Ally prompts. "Then what?"

"Veronica and I became friends. I took her under my wing, showed her around the school." Lilith rolls her eyes. "But that didn't work out."

"Why not?" Wes asks.

"I kept going over the Glinda parts with her, but every time I left the music room, she'd be practicing 'Over the Rainbow'! I finally just told her, 'That's *my* part. Mr. Ackins told me.' And then Veronica says"—Lilith's voice goes super high and syrupy—"'Mr. Ackins told me auditions were in two weeks and that all parts are open.'"

"What'd you do?" Ally asks.

"Well, I went straight to Mr. Ackins, of course. I told him he had to let the rest of the class know that the lead was taken but that auditions would be open for the other parts. He told me I'd audition like everyone else."

"That kind of sounds fair," Rex says.

Lilith holds her head high. "Yes and I signed up to audition. Like everyone else. The only other person trying out for Dorothy was, of course, pretty, perfect Veronica." Lilith thinks about how Veronica came in with a cluster of giggling girls and goofing-off boys to cheer her on.

Lilith's chin pops up a little higher. "I worked so hard. I was *good*, like really good." She swallows. "I nailed the song. For a minute after I sang, no one said anything. Then everyone—every-one—applauded. Even the stupid girls who came in with Veronica clapped. But Mr. Ackins? He didn't even look up. Not once, during the whole performance did he even *look* at me."

"You were amazing," Jason says.

"You were—"

"Yeah," Jason cuts her off. "I was there."

Lilith mouths *thank you* to Jason. "Anyway, Veronica was next. She walked onto the stage, and the spotlight did look good on her. I'll admit it. And she sang. She had to hold the script to get the words right, and she still flubbed a couple lines—like she said *dumdrops* instead of *gumdrops*. Little stuff like that."

Jason nods. "Yeah, she was okay."

"Right!" Lilith slaps her knee. "She was okay. But she wasn't me. I was better than she was. I'm not trying to be a snob or a jerk. I was better than her because I had worked harder. I knew the part. I went to voice lessons. I *earned* it.

"From the side of the stage, I had a perfect vantage point to watch both Veronica and Mr. Ackins. He put down the notebook when she took the stage. He crossed his hands behind his head and watched her with a big stupid smile on his face. When she finished, he turned to the group of kids she had arrived with—the *cool* kids—and gave them a thumbs-up. But I thought, again, that he was just being nice. There was *no way* I wasn't going to get the part."

Lilith swallows. "The next day, the list was posted outside the auditorium. I didn't even have to walk up to it. As soon as I came close, everyone stopped talking. They parted for me like it was a red carpet event or something. And there next to Dorothy's name was Veronica's. I ran my finger down the list, seeing where I'd be. I think I was sort of numb. I started thinking about Glinda, about how she's really the catalyst for the play. She even costars in *Wicked*, right? And at least I'd still having a singing role. But I never made it down the list to Glinda's name because I saw it: I was Auntie Em. *Auntie Em.*"

"That's cold, man," Wes says.

Lilith swipes at a tear on her cheek. "I'm not crying because I'm sad. I'm crying because I'm angry. Just so you know."

Ally's hand darts out and closes over Lilith's hand. Lilith sighs and shakes off Ally's hand.

"I went to Mr. Ackins right away. I said it wasn't fair—that I deserved a bigger role. He said it was time to give someone else a shot—that I took up too much space onstage."

"Too much space?" Ally asks. "Like metaphorically or something?"

Lilith rolls her eyes. She shifts a little. "That's what I thought. But then he, like, looked at me. At my . . . middle."

"But you're not . . ." Ally stops.

Lilith sighs. "I'm soft figured. That's how I like to think of it. I have, like, hips and stuff. And I *like* how I look. But if I were bigger, who cares? Who freaking cares? My teacher certainly shouldn't."

"What a jerk," Rex mutters. She scoots a little closer to Lilith.

"What did you do?" Wes asks.

"What could I do? I became Auntie Em. And I was awesome at it." Lilith looks away. "And, all right, maybe I did take a little pleasure in Veronica messing up her lines. She couldn't figure out the skip *at all*. But I never said anything. She even asked me for help a couple of times. 'Lily, my background is in television,' she'd say. Seriously! And, being Auntie Em, I gave her tips. You know, stuff like how to breathe during the songs so she didn't gasp for air in between stanzas.

"The whole time, Mr. Ackins was so stinking . . . I don't know, *superior* about the whole thing. 'Oh, Veronica, you're just a natural onstage!' and 'It's so *refreshing* to hear a subtle take on these songs.' It felt humiliating to me and how I'd been trying to perform."

"If it's any consolation," Jason says, "he also found ways to jab

239

at Pedro and the kid playing the Scarecrow. Mr. Ackins told him to stop trying so hard to portray someone without a brain. I overhead him say, 'Just be yourself.'"

Rex winces. "Wow."

"Yeah," Jason says. "Maybe Mrs. Wahlberg can find one of those private school gigs for him next year and trade places."

Wes rubs at the back of his head.

"Anyway," Lilith says, "a day before the show, we had dress rehearsal. And I think up until that moment, I hadn't really felt sad about the whole thing. Just angry. Like I felt cheated out of the spot, but I wasn't hurt all that much. Until that day.

"I think it was the set. The beginning scenes—with Kansas—were all painted in black, whites, and grays. The cornfield was painted in a way that made it seem to go on forever. That doesn't even really do it justice. It was sad. Like, the backdrop just had so much loneliness and sadness sketched into it.

"And then, when the stage became Oz, the magic and wonder . . . it was just beautiful." Lilith pauses, trying to think of the right way to describe what it had looked like. The yellow brick road stretched across the stage. Munchkinland was as bright and cheerful as her baby sister's first laugh. The backdrop during the apple tree scene—where Dorothy realizes the trees are alive—featured hundreds of tiny glow-in-the-dark eyes that shimmered under the stage lights between long, stretching dark shadows. The

Wicked Witch's castle wasn't just creepy; it was ominous.

Lilith looks around the group. Rex, Wes, and Ally are watching her, waiting for her to go on. Jason listens, too, even though his head is ducked under his hand. "I can't do it justice. Anyone could've been Dorothy on that set. I would've kicked butt on that stage. But Veronica? Ugh." Lilith's fingers curl into fists again. "She couldn't get through one scene—*one scene*—without standing in front of someone, stealing their line, or forgetting her own. It was awful. Tickets were sold out, and she couldn't even remember her lines!"

"Sold out?" Ally says. "Weren't tickets free?"

Lilith ignores her. "Mr. Ackins asked her to practice more, to study the script. He had folks making little cue cards to hold up if she needed them. Totally amateur. Even he, I think, figured out by then that Veronica was more Glinda than main star material."

"Glen the Good Witch did a good job, though," Jason says.

Lilith shrugs. "He was okay. Anyway, that was Thursday. Our show was supposed to be Friday night. Friday morning, I was backstage helping the makeup crew figure out how to make Pedro a mustache that would match the lion's mane. I heard Veronica come in, again surrounded by her crowd of friends." Lilith crosses her arms. "Digression here, but how in the world did she get so many friends so quickly? She'd been there seven weeks!"

Rex sighs. "Some people are like friend magnets." Wes smiles full dimple and winks. Rex's groan dissolves into a laugh.

"Anyway, she and her friends go backstage, and I sneak away from the makeup crew to hear what's going on. Veronica goes to Mr. Ackins and says she's just 'not feeling it.' Mr. Ackins tells her she has to do the show; she's the lead. Veronica tells him that her mom and dad are taking her to meet with a talent agent in Hollywood, and they're leaving right after school. 'My future is on the small screen,' she says. And Mr. Ackins? He *wishes her well*. Honestly, he says it's a shame she won't be in the play, but he wishes her well."

Lilith throws up her hands. She shifts her body position so her knees are under her, even though it messes up her dress. "I waited a couple minutes. Then I went to Mr. Ackins. He was on the stage. No one was around, except for someone adding a few more details to the Oz backdrop. I said to Mr. Ackins, 'Hey, I just heard about Veronica. I know the play by heart. I can be Dorothy.' Perfect solution, right? Wrong. Mr. Ackins just looked at me like I was a dead bug or something. 'No, thanks,' he said. 'No way we can make so many changes so quickly. You'll all get passing grades for drama, but we're canceling the play. I've already contacted the principal.'

"Then he called everyone to the stage. He thanked them for their dedication and told them that due to unforeseen circumstances, they wouldn't be putting on the show after all. 'But you all should be very proud of the hard work you've done.' Puke. Then someone shouted, 'The show must go on!'"

"That was you," Jason says. "*You* were the one who shouted that."

Lilith continues, ignoring Jason's comment. "Mr. Ackins just wished everyone a good summer—that's it." Her fists open and close, over and over. "I went back to his office. I was going to talk some sense into him. I mean, all those tickets we sold!"

"But weren't they free?" Wes says.

"I know the tickets were free! *That's not the point!*" Lilith screeches.

They pause while they hear Mr. Hardy's heavy footsteps across the hall. "What's going on?" he barks into the room.

"Nothing," they all say together.

He gestures with two fingers to his eyes, then two fingers to them, and returns to the office across the hall.

Lilith takes a deep breath and huffs it out through her nose. "I was going to tell him that we deserved to have a play—that we had all worked so hard. I mean, if you could've seen that set. Even the art club went above and beyond to make it just glow!"

"Even the art club," Jason echoes.

"You know what I mean," Lilith says. "But he was on the phone. 'Hey, babe,' he said. 'I'm free tonight after all.' He told the person—his girlfriend, I guess—that he wasn't doing the play after all because the lead quit. 'Yeah, there's an understudy, I guess,' he said. 'There's a girl who'd pull it off, no sweat. Honestly, she's a heck of a lot better than the girl who got the part.' He laughed, then said, 'But no way am I letting that full-of-herself brat get the spotlight. You know the type. Total pain-in-the-butt know-it-all who thinks she's a star, when the truth is, she's a total bore.'"

"Oooooh," Wes says softly. "Ouch."

Ally reaches out and squeezes Lilith's hand again. This time she doesn't shake it off.

"He turned around then. He *saw* me. Do you think he looked ashamed of himself? No. He rolled his eyes. *He rolled his eyes.* I guess I . . . I sort of lost it. I whipped around, right into someone—I didn't even see whoever it was, but I know I knocked him down—and then I was suddenly on the stage."

Lilith stands and faces the wall, away from the group. "It's okay if people don't like me. I'm not easy to like. I know that. I've always known that. But that doesn't mean I don't feel things. It doesn't mean I don't deserve what I work hard to get. I . . . I lost it. Everything I always bottle up—everything. Do you know how many people roll their eyes at me every day? Do you think any of them—any of *you*—understand how hard it is to want to be anyone other than who you are?"

"Why wouldn't you want to be you?" Ally asks.

"Because I'm boring!" Lilith shouts into the wall. "I'm bor-ing, okay! If I'm not being Lilith the drama queen"—she turns and stretches her arms—"then I'm a nobody. If I'm Lilith the actress, it doesn't hurt that no one will sit with me at lunch. Because they're all just jealous of my potential, right? If people roll their eyes and call me dramatic, it's fine because I'm *trying* to be dramatic. It doesn't hurt."

Rex stands, too. She faces Lilith. "It hurts anyway."

"So I freaked out. I didn't even know I was doing it," Lilith says, letting tears fall down her cheeks. "The whole set—that gorgeous, incredible set—I ripped it apart. I stomped on it, flipped it, trashed it. I don't know what I was thinking. I wasn't thinking! And then, suddenly, it's like I woke up. And the whole drama team was surrounding the stage. They were laughing at me. They were rolling their eyes. Someone said, 'At least we got a show after all.' Mr. Ackins was there, too. He shook his head. He rolled his eyes. Again. And then I was in Mr. Hardy's room—I don't remember how I got there."

Lilith sinks to the ground and buries her face in her propped-up knees.

"So that's the whole story."

None of them say anything for a moment. Finally, softly, Lilith adds, "I wish I had apologized to the set designers. They must've spent months on the set."

"Don't worry about it," Jason says.

"What?" Lilith looks up at him.

"It only took a few weeks. I got a lot of pictures of the set, so I can still use them in my portfolio to get into honors art this year. Where would I keep scenes from Oz after the play anyway?"

"The design was yours?" Lilith gasps.

"Yeah, it wasn't so much the 'art club' or 'set designers.' It was just me." Jason scratches his chin and smiles softly at Lilith. "I don't blame you. That freak-out? It was epic. It was, I don't know. I wish I had done it." He laughs. "I don't blame you," he says again. "I blame Mr. Ackins. But don't worry. I got my revenge."

3:17 p.m.

JASON "The Nobody"

"You're up, Picasso," Rex says.

Jason shrugs. "It's not—"

"*A big deal*," the other four finish.

"Yeah, we know." Wes laughs. "Spill anyway."

Jason glances at Lilith, who is watching him with wide eyes. "I was there," he says, "that whole semester, working on the set design for the play." He scratches the back of his neck. "My dad, he's always getting on my case about being off by myself, being a loner. He *really* means a nobody. He signed me up to be on the drama team." In a booming voice, Jason imitates his dad: "'If you're not going to do sports, you've got to do something.' I don't think he knew that once I signed up, I could do something other than act. And the art teacher was bugging me to get a portfolio together for high school honors art. So I offered to do the set design. I did all of the artwork for the show." His cheeks flame. "When the others saw my sketches, everyone else joined other crews, like costume or makeup."

"Because you're awesome," Rex adds.

Jason's face turns a deeper red. "Whatever. But, like, I have this thing. When I was a kid, I thought of it as a superpower, I guess. Only it's pretty much the worst superpower ever. I can disappear. I can be right in front of people and their eyes slide right on by me like I don't exist. That's how it was with Mr. Ackins. I'd be working on the design and hear him say these awful things— to you, Lilith, and lots of other people, too." Jason's jaw clenches. "And I didn't do anything about it."

"What could you have done?" Rex asks.

"I could've done *something*." Jason stares down at his knees. "My dad and Mr. Ackins would get along great. My dad is awesome at sharpening words and stabbing me with them." His voice booms again: "'Carla, look! Kid's hair's longer than yours. Didn't you always want a girl?' Things like that, you know. Focusing on how I'm not, like . . . well, not like Ally in sports or Wes in social situations."

Rex motions to Jason. "You said something about revenge?"

"Right." Jason halfway smiles. "It's kind of lame."

The other four groan. "Come on, already!"

"Well, Mr. Ackins. He'd say all sorts of awful things to kids, not knowing or caring that I was there. Like that stuff to Pedro, about not fitting in the costume? That was nothing." Jason shook his head. "Pedro told him he'd work on the skipping scene at home—remember he had trouble getting that down?" Jason says to Lilith, who nods. "Mr. Ackins said, 'I'd be happier if you skipped the second helpings this weekend' and then puffed up his cheeks. Like you said, he had his favorites, and he'd let them say anything about anyone and just laugh. Or he'd add to the mockery and cover it with their laughter."

Jason turns to Rex. "I was in class when he did that to you, Rex—with the thing about the lice." He stares down at his knees again. "I wrote it down. All the awful things he said. I wrote them in my sketchbook. I don't know why, but I couldn't help it."

Jason peeks at Rex. "This next part kind of involves you."

Rex's forehead wrinkles. She sinks to the floor, her eyes on Jason.

"I was in the hall once, and you were there. Ahead of you, that kid, Winston, was getting picked on." Jason glances at Wes. "By Ashley."

"Ashley's a jerk," Wes says.

"Then why is he your friend?" Rex counters.

Wes looks away. "Maybe he won't be for long."

"Ashley was trying to get Winston to give up his Algebra homework," Jason says. "He was like, 'Come on, geek! Are you going to make me beat it out of you?' Saying stuff like that."

"I remember this," says Rex, smiling.

Jason smiles back. "Yeah. You just walked up and stood behind Winston, holding up your phone like you were recording. Winston didn't even know you were there. But Ashley did. And he told Winston, 'Never mind, dork. I'll do it myself.'" Jason laughs. "All you did was stand there. It sort of clicked. People will say all sorts of things if no one else is listening—if no one *does* anything about it.

"So that morning, when Mr. Ackins said all of those things about you, Lilith, I heard them. What he said on the phone— the way he looked at you afterward. I was there after Mr. Hardy ordered you to his office, when he asked Mr. Ackins what was going on. 'Kid's crazy,' Mr. Ackins had said. 'She's a drama queen, what do you expect?'

"Mr. Hardy glared at him. Like, I mean, bushy eyebrows confess-your-sins Hardy glare."

"I'm familiar with it," Rex says.

"We all are," Wes pipes in.

"I knew then that Mr. Hardy was onto him, but what could Hardy do when no one ever heard the things Ackins said? No one ever made him face his words." Jason pauses. "Mr. Hardy told Ackins to go to his office, too. I started to write down what he had said in my sketchbook. But it was like the words were too big or something.

"I had these black spray paint bottles for the set design. I shoved them into my bag, and I went to the parking lot." Jason stares at his hands. "Mr. Ackins's car is white. It *was* white, I mean."

"No way!" Lilith gasps.

Jason takes a deep breath. "It was so stupid—I could've gotten in so much trouble. I mean, I *did* get into a lot of trouble. I sprayed the whole car with his own words. I wish I would've gotten a picture of it before the police arrived. For my portfolio, I mean."

He looks up at the rest of them. They're all staring, not blinking or moving.

"I'm just joking. I didn't do it."

Wes falls to his side with a groan. Rex laughs and shakes her head. Lilith balls up a piece of notebook paper and nails Jason in the head with it.

Ally just shakes her head. "Why didn't you? That would have been so perfect."

Jason takes a big breath. "There was a car seat in the back of his car. Did you know he's a dad? So, I pulled out the papers instead. I told you that I wrote the words, but I sketched the people, too. Just their eyes, I mean. I sketched their eyes when they heard him say those things. I went back into the school. I went to the copier room—I told you, I can be, like, invisible. No one stopped me. I made forty stapled copies. And then I went around the school. I put a copy on every teacher's desk. I put the rest in the teacher's lounge. And then I went home.

"Mr. Hardy showed up at my house that night with the booklet." Jason shakes his head. "He told my parents he thought I had done outstanding work on an art project. My dad was floored. He then asked me to be part of an anti-bullying campaign at the high school this year. I'm supposed to recruit all of you."

Jason ignores a second balled-up paper shot to the head.

"That's why you're here?" Wes says. "To recruit us into some stupid little club?"

Jason shrugs. "I guess. I mean, Mr. Hardy made it really clear that I'm here because I shouldn't have used office supplies. But I think the club is the real reason. He told me to figure out a way to talk to you guys about it today."

"I am *not* going around school telling people to be nice to each other and tattling on bullies," Rex says. "That's like putting a giant target on your back."

"Yeah, no, thank you," Lilith adds. "I already have no friends."

"Exactly," Rex says.

"That's not true," Ally says. She gets up and stands between the two of them.

"So we're, like, friends now?" Rex says with a scowl on her face.

Ally shrugs. "Why not?"

"Yeah." Rex snorts. "Sit together at lunch. Save a spot for Amelia. We'll paint our nails and have sleepovers."

Wes and Jason glance at each other. "I'm not going to paint your nails, man."

Jason grins and wiggles his fingers at Wes. The nails are inked black with Sharpie. "No need."

Lilith crosses her arms. "I will. If any of you want to sit with me at lunch, that's cool with me." She narrows her eyes at Ally. "Even you."

Ally smiles. "That sounds nice."

No one says anything for a minute. Wes stares at his fingers. "Yeah, okay," he says eventually. "I'll say hi to you guys in the hall."

"Oh, wow," Rex says and fans herself with her hand. "The great Wes will say *hi to me in the hall*? Picasso, this club of yours is working already."

"That's not what I meant!" Wes says. He throws his head back. "I'm going to try to change, okay? I just don't want to be like, 'oh, yeah, sure, we'll all be besties now.' I don't know what high school's going to be like. None of us do! All I know is I'm off student council. Mr. Hardy told me when I got this detention. I'm going to have to figure stuff out. Figure out who I want to be. And, yeah, it'd be cool if we all could hang out again. But I don't know."

"I was thinking about that. What if it isn't a club for kids?" Jason says. "What if it's a club for teachers?"

"Seriously?" Rex asks.

Jason nods. "Yeah, like we'd talk to teachers. Mr. Hardy said I could structure it however I want, so maybe we say it has to start with us telling teachers what we need first, how they should handle things, what they should say."

"Well, this club thing explains a couple of things," Lilith says. "Like why Mr. Hardy was leaving us alone so much all day. He was giving you space to recruit us."

"Stupid, huh?" Jason says. "Why would he put me in charge? I'm no leader. I'm a nobody."

"Yeah, and I'm just a flirt." Wes crosses his arms.

"And I'm the drama queen," Lilith murmurs.

"Just an athlete," Ally adds.

"Rebel over here," Rex finishes. She leans forward and joke-punches Jason in the shoulder. "You've led us all day. You just didn't know it."

"Yeah, it was pretty annoying, actually," Lilith says.

Rex laughs. "You know what's funny? All of you guys are here, and *I'm* the one everyone thinks of as a bully. But each of you is here because you tried to—or did—push someone into doing what you wanted." She shakes her head.

No one says anything for a minute. Then Ally slowly says, "Why *are* you here, Rex?"

"Do you even have to ask? Aren't I like *known* for being in trouble?" Rex says, a smirk on her face.

Ally raises an eyebrow.

"What?" Rex says.

Lilith shifts to sit cross-legged on the floor. "Well, you've been tracking TBN for six months."

"I told you—Mr. Hardy is giving me detention—"

"All the time, yeah," Wes says. "But Mrs. Mitchell said it's the first time she's had kids here."

Rex pulls her phone out of her pocket and checks the time. "Guys, we have less than twenty minutes until we have to do this stupid skit. We've got, like, nothing."

"That's not true," Ally says. "Lilith told us she has the whole *Wizard of Oz* down. Here's your chance." Ally smiles at Lilith.

"I don't know . . . ," she says, swaying back and forth a little and fluffing her dress.

Wes winks at the rest of them. "Or we could—"

"Oh, all right! All right," Lilith says. "I'll do it."

"And what about the essay, the one that Mr. Hardy expects us to write?" Rex points out.

Jason holds up his sketchbook. "Got it covered. So long as you guys are, you know, in the club."

He hands Rex the sketchbook. The other three gather around her to read the essay.

"Wow, man," Wes says. "This is perfect." He grabs the pencil from behind Jason's ear and signs the essay. Passing the pencil around, they each sign it.

"I don't think Mr. Hardy's going to like it," Rex says.

"Who cares? It's honest," Ally says. "So that's taken care of. And we have plenty of time for your story, Rex."

Rex grabs a fistful of her hair and tugs. "Not much to tell, is there? I had to be here today, just like you guys."

"But why?" Lilith asks.

Quieter, Jason says, "You can tell us."

Rex's jaw flexes. "What did Mr. Hardy tell you, Jason?"

Jason scoots back a little. "Nothing." He looks at his feet. "People say things around me, and I hear rumors."

"Then why are you asking me this? What do you know?"

Jason shakes his head again. "I don't know anything. Not really. Except you were surprised to see the rest of us here today, but Mrs. Mitchell and Mr. Hardy weren't surprised to see you."

"I know your mom left your family more than a year ago," Wes says. He looks down at his hands then back up at Rex. "I know about ten months ago, something happened that made you different. I think it's whatever happened to your brother."

Ally quietly adds, "I know you wanted us to stay off of the third

256

floor." She looks up at Rex. "What happened to August?"

Rex starts to answer. "He—"

Mr. Hardy opens the door. "All right, students. We're almost at the end of our day." He gives Jason a long look. "Have you come to any conclusions?"

Jason nods and looks to the others. "I told them about the anti-bullying club."

Mr. Hardy crosses his arms. "And?"

"Why would you want us in it?" Wes asks. "I mean, you know what we did."

"Exactly," Mr. Hardy says. "I know what you did. I also know what you're capable of doing."

Mrs. Mitchell's quick footsteps *tap, tap, tap* down the hall. "We're ready for you, students! The residents are assembling in the main room. Let's make this short and sweet, shall we?"

"We've decided to go in a classic direction," Lilith says. "Acting out bits of *The Wizard of Oz*."

Mrs. Mitchell crosses her arms. "Your original piece that you've spent the past hour on is *The Wizard of Oz*?"

Lilith nods. "We'll be performing it in an original way."

"Right," Mrs. Mitchell says in a clipped voice.

Mr. Hardy holds out his hand. "I'll collect your essays now. I assume they focus on the anti-bullying initiative?"

The five of them exchange a look. Each nods to Jason and he

tears out the piece of paper, handing the essay to Mr. Hardy. The principal glances at it and then back up at them. "Listen—"

But before he can speak, the walkie-talkie on Mrs. Mitchell's hip buzzes. "Code Blue! Code Blue! We have a Code Blue on the third level! Emergency physicians, all available hands, report to the third level!"

"What's a Code Blue?" Lilith asks.

"Someone's dying!" Rex gasps and pushes past them. She tears off down the hall, Mr. Hardy and Mrs. Mitchell calling after her.

Wes grabs Jason's arm. "Hubert!" he says. "What if it's Hubert? He was going to have to move to the third floor. What if he already did? And Grace is still mad at him!" Wes sprints from the room, heading in the opposite direction of Rex.

Ally whispers, "I don't think Rex should be going up there alone." She turns to Jason and looks at him straight on. "August is on the third floor, isn't he?"

Jason ducks his head, then nods. "I think so."

"You've thought so from the beginning, haven't you?"

He nods again.

"What happened to him?" Ally asks. "You know, don't you?"

"I heard a rumor."

Jason turns away as Lilith peeks out the door. "Hardy and Mitchell just chased Rex. Wes is headed the other way. Let's go.

258

Now, before they come back for us. You know they're not going to catch those guys. But maybe we can."

Jason says, "But what about the—"

"It's just a stupid skit," Lilith says, already kicking off her platform sandals. "Let's go!"

Jason trails behind the other two as they dart up the stairs, taking them two or three at a time as they race to get to the third floor. As they pass doorways, they hear more walkie-talkies ringing out.

Reaching the third floor at last, they burst through the doors. Mr. Hardy and Mrs. Mitchell stand in front of them with their backs turned.

"Crap," Lilith mutters and lets the door ease shut. They peek through the rectangle window on the door. Mr. Hardy has his hand on Rex's shoulder, whose back also is to them. Mrs. Mitchell stands on her other side. They're leading her away from a room as several nurses and doctors trickle from it. Everyone is moving slowly, shoulders slumped, not at all like the rush to get to the room. Rex turns and they can see her profile.

She nods and smiles up at Mr. Hardy. Lilith quietly opens the door a crack. "Thank you," Rex says. "I guess I . . . I sort of panicked when I heard 'third floor.'"

"Yes, dear," Mrs. Mitchell says. "But the third floor is where stuff like this happens. You know that. Everything is fine."

"For now," Rex says. Mr. Hardy squeezes her shoulder. She moves away from his grip, and his hand falls to his side.

"Yes," Mrs. Mitchell says and exchanges a glance with Mr. Hardy over Rex's downturned head. "For now."

3:42 p.m.

WES "The Flirt"

The conference room where the group has spent the past hour and a half is smack in the middle of the floor with a stairway at both ends. Wes sprints so fast his arms are pumping. At the staircase, he barrels up half a flight of stairs before he hears it.

Kissing. Like loud, movie star kissing echoing down the staircase to him from above. *Ew.* Wes shudders.

Now what? He could keep on running, make sure Hubert is okay, but he'd have to get past whoever was making out in the staircase. Just how much longer would the elevator be? Finally, there's a pause in the kissing and Wes hears, "Hubbie, if you had just told me the truth!"

Hubbie? Wes trots up the stairs. Grace and Hubert pull apart from their embrace and gasp at Wes, who bends, clutches his knees, and laughs.

"What on earth are you doing here, Wes?" Grace asks. She fans at her cheeks.

Wes laughs as Hubert's face turns a deep shade of red. "I heard the alarms. Wanted to make sure you were okay. That if it was you, Grace knew, too."

"Wait," Grace says, stepping back from Hubert. "Wes knows? About the congestive heart failure?"

Wes shakes his head. "No, I just figured it out on my own."

Grace pats Hubert's cheek. "I wish I would've sooner."

Hubert shoves his hands into his pockets. "I was a fool, Gracie. I should've told you from the get-go, but I wanted to spare you the pain. Wes here helped me figure out I was just hurting you more." He pulls his wife closer to him. "And the truth is, I don't want to do this alone."

"You won't have to."

Wes looks away as they kiss again. He clears his throat and they laugh, pulling apart. Grace sighs. "Thank you, Wes, for convincing this stubborn old man to see reason." To Hubert, she adds, "I wouldn't have traded my past for anything, but I do wish I would've had more time with you. Could've traveled the world."

"Taken you to Paris. Or even dancing," Hubert says.

Wes shrugs. "Well, I'm going to prom here with Judith on Saturday. You two should join me. Maybe we could talk Mrs. Mitchell into putting up a disco ball and playing some tunes for us." Wes grins. "I know a couple kids I bet would help out."

Hubert and Grace laugh in unison. "Deal," Hubert says.

As the couple put their arms around each other again, swaying back and forth as Hubert sings into Grace's ear, Wes backtracks down the stairs. He heads to the conference room, sees that it's empty, and starts running again, this time to the other stairway.

At the top of the third floor stairs, he pauses again, this time taking in the backs of his friends, all of whom are clustered around the cracked-open door, clearly eavesdropping. He tiptoes forward. "What are we listening to?" he whispers.

"Gah!" Lilith gasps. Jason, Ally, and Lilith duck down from the door window. Wes catches a glimpse of Mr. Hardy and Mrs. Mitchell talking with Rex before they turn toward the door.

A second later, the four of them tumble into the hall when the stairwell door is yanked open. "As I was saying, Rex," Mr. Hardy booms, "I don't think you have to go back to the others. I had a feeling they'd be on their way to you." He crosses his arms as the quartet stand.

Lilith straightens her dress. "We were just—"

"Save it," Mr. Hardy says. "Back to the conference room." He holds open the door. Softer, he adds, "Rex, if you want to make sure everything is good with your own eyes, I understand."

Rex stares down at her feet and then up at the four of them.

Just then a nurse steps out of the room near where they stood. Doctors and nurses had been rushing in and out of the room, but now it was quiet. "Not long now," the nurse whispers to Mrs. Mitchell. "But Frank's still asking for his granddaughter."

Mrs. Mitchell shakes her head. "Even if she left now, Becky would never get here in time."

Lilith gasps. She glances back at the rest of them with wide eyes and then goes into the room.

"Stop!" Mrs. Mitchell says. "You can't go in there!"

But Lilith doesn't stop. A chair is beside the bed. She pulls it closer and slips her hand under the palm of the old man's.

"Becky?" Frank, the old man, whispers.

Lilith glances at Mrs. Mitchell, whose eyes fill with tears.

"Becky?" Frank says again.

"Hi, Pap," Lilith says, her voice coming out in a squeak.

Frank smiles. "Becky girl!" Each word is a whisper with a long pause between.

"Want me to sing for you, Pap?" Lilith asks. She doesn't notice as the others gather in the doorway.

"Is this appropriate?" Mr. Hardy asks Mrs. Mitchell as she steps away from the room.

Mrs. Mitchell shakes her head. "Of course not. But that doesn't

264

mean it isn't right."

Lilith is crying as she sings about waking with clouds far behind her, and as Frank's eyes slowly close.

"Is he gone?" Lilith whispers after the song ends.

Mrs. Mitchell shakes her head. She lays her hand on Lilith's shoulder, squeezing gently, as she points to the machine showing Frank's heartbeat. "He's here; he's just peaceful right now."

Mrs. Mitchell holds out her hand but Lilith shakes her head.

"I don't want to leave him alone."

Mrs. Mitchell smiles in a sad way. "He won't be, dear," she says, but not in a fake, folksy way. "Not for a moment. We'll be with him the whole time." As if on cue, a nurse quietly enters the room. Mrs. Mitchell gently leads Lilith to the others.

Without hesitating, Ally pulls Lilith into a hug. Jason pats the back of her head. Wes shoves his hands in his pockets, but moves closer to them. Only Rex stands slightly to the side. They stand like this until Lilith's breath steadies. When Lilith pulls away, her eyes are red.

"Are you okay?" Ally asks.

"Of course not," Lilith answers.

No one speaks for a long moment.

"Would you, guys . . . ," Rex says in a voice so low she is surprised to see them each look her way. She takes a deeper breath. "Would you, guys, want to meet August?"

REX "The Rebel"
or
Just REX

Rex orders her arms to stop shaking. Orders her voice to be loud.

"My brother." Her chin pops up. "Do you want to meet him?"

It was stupid to think of August—*August*—as a secret.

August was never a whisper. His was the name she shouted as she opened the door at the end of the day; the name she called from the kitchen table when she couldn't figure out a math problem; the name she screamed when she was lost in a crowd.

But somehow *August* had gotten stuck in the filter of her lips, ever since that terrible day when she first realized that it didn't matter how much you love a person. It didn't matter if his face was the one that anchored you in place. It didn't matter if you *needed* him. Love isn't a strong enough glue to keep a person together, and it will smash you to bits if you try.

She hadn't said his name out loud—hadn't even *thought* it—since then. Until this morning, shoveling tuna casserole with Picasso. With Jason.

Ally walks beside Rex. Lilith treads by her other side, with Jason and Wes just behind them. Farther back, Mr. Hardy and Mrs. Mitchell trail the group. As they walk, Rex finally talks about her brother. "August, he always took care of me. Earlier, I said he took care of me after Mom left, but that's not true. He's always taken care of me, even before she left. Far back as I can remember, he's the one who would check my homework, tuck me in at night, make me breakfast." Rex stares straight ahead, every so often peeking to the side where Ally watches her face. "So it wasn't a big deal to me when she bailed. I still had him."

Rex rakes her hand through her choppy hair, then continues. "But I didn't think about what it was like for August. He was—*is*—a lot older than me. He was twenty-two when Mom left, and he still lived with us. I thought he was so strong. So able to handle anything and everything. I've always been . . . I worry that I'm a lot like Mom. She, like, blows up at people. She's selfish. She can totally cut a person up or rip them apart just with what she says.

But August wasn't—isn't—anything like that. He's kind, and quiet, and thoughtful. Pulls-up-the-blankets-at-night thoughtful. And so I'd just tell myself that what made him made me, too."

"What about your dad?" Lilith asks. "Where is he?"

Rex shakes her head. "He died when I was a little kid. Car accident."

Ally puts her hand on Rex's shoulder. Rex shrugs it off, but then she smiles at Ally. "Sorry. I just don't like . . ."

Ally nods and she laughs. "I don't, either. Not usually. Don't know what's going on with me today."

Rex sends her a halfway smile. "I don't think any of us do."

"What happened when your mom left? To August, I mean?" Wes asks.

Rex swallows. "Nothing at first. Mom left a lot, but she usually came back after a couple days. But when weeks went by without hearing from her, August changed. He didn't eat as much as he should've. He didn't sleep at night. He got fired from his job as an apprentice for a carpenter."

Ally nods. "My dad changed, too, when Mom left. He got, I don't know, more focused. More intense."

"It was the opposite for August," Rex says. "I'd come home and he'd still be in his pajamas. I started making dinners. He didn't even do things he used to love, like playing the guitar or listening to music. He . . . he kind of checked out."

"Was he sick?" Wes asks.

Rex doesn't say anything. She glances over her shoulder at Mr. Hardy. He lifts his head in a half nod and says, "Not all sicknesses are visible or as easily understood. August was hurting. He was depressed. Would you say that's right, Rex?"

Rex nods once, a quick duck of her head. "He'd say things like how I deserved more, deserved to be with a real family. How he was worthless."

Lilith shifts closer to Rex, but is careful not to touch her.

"Rex . . . ," Mr. Hardy says, but she shakes her head, swallows.

"August took a lot of pills one day. There was a note, with our grandmother's phone number and address written on it."

No one says anything. Rex's face burns.

In the thick silence, Mrs. Mitchell clears her throat. With a strong voice, she says, "Doctors were able to revive him, but he hadn't had enough oxygen for a really long time. When a brain is deprived of oxygen, it becomes damaged. Most of the time that damage is not reversible."

"What does that mean?" Ally asks, her eyes darting from Rex to Mr. Hardy to Mrs. Mitchell. But Rex stops walking abruptly. On the door next to where she stops is a picture of the resident, just like in the other halls. This time, though, it isn't an old woman or man. Pictured is a young man with thick dark hair, wide brown eyes, and the same heart-shaped face as Rex.

Her chin high, Rex glowers at them, daring them to keep walking. Daring them to stay.

Wes and Jason file past her into the room.

Rex raises her eyebrow at Ally, taking in the shimmer of sweat breaking out over her forehead.

Lilith's jaw sets. She narrows her eyes, then puts her arm around Ally's waist. "I'm going to help you be strong now," she whispers, "and you're going to help me later."

"About Frank?" Ally asks.

Lilith nods. She leads Ally into the room.

Mr. Hardy and Mrs. Mitchell hang back. Mrs. Mitchell reaches toward Rex, but she backsteps before she can touch her.

"Hi, August." *Good job,* she tells herself when her voice comes out sounding solid and controlled. Rex crosses the room on steady legs to where her brother sits in a large black wheelchair. His arms are curled at his side and his face hollow, more so even than it is in the picture on the door. His mouth stretches in a lopsided smile. "I brought some friends today."

The four glance at one another, and then Wes steps forward. "Hey, man," he says. "Nice to meet you. I'm Wes."

Wes's voice isn't any different when he talks to her brother than to other people, and it makes her so grateful that she smiles straight at him for the first time all day. Some people, even some nurses, have super high voices when they talk to August. It gets under Rex's skin. *He's still a grown man, not a baby,* she tells them. But she doesn't have to with Wes. He looks at August, too, when he talks to him. Not everyone does that, either.

The other three stand against the far wall. Rex sits on the bed next to the wheelchair and turns to the group. Jaw set, she says, "He can't talk anymore." She glances at Mrs. Mitchell, who's still in the doorway with Mr. Hardy.

Mrs. Mitchell nods. "Rex believes he understands, though. And we think he might know more than we give him credit for. Don't you, love?"

"He can't walk." Rex points to the wheelchair. "Or feed himself. Or . . ."

As her voice trails off, Lilith walks to the window. "Maybe you'd like some sunshine in here, August?" She pulls open the curtains. "Oh, look!" She holds up the album next to the record player beneath the window. "My parents love the Beatles."

"August does, too," Rex says.

Lilith turns on the player, to a song about a yellow submarine. She sings along, and it's probably just the sunlight, but for a moment the room seems to glow yellow.

"Hey," Ally says, moving away from the wall toward August. Her cheeks are two red splotches on her face. "His mouth is moving!" She swallows. "I mean, are you singing along, August?"

Rex nods. "Like I said, he can't talk. But he likes music. He remembers lyrics."

Ally smiles, her eyes on August's face. Her smile is shaky, like she doesn't know if she's doing the right thing. Rex looks away, but then Ally says, "I don't sing out loud, either. My name's Ally, by the way."

A soft noise rumbles out of August. His hand jerks outward toward Ally. She reaches for it instead of stepping away, taking his arm and standing closer to him. "I'm happy to meet you, August."

There aren't any more places to sit in the room, now that Ally is in the chair next to August, and Wes and Rex are both sitting on the bed. Lilith is perched on the counter under the window, next to the record player. So Jason sinks to the ground and pulls out his sketchbook. "Do you mind if I draw you guys?"

Wes shows Rex a picture on his phone of Hubert and Grace hugging in the stairway. "True love."

Rex shrugs. "I'm not convinced, Wes."

"Not yet, anyway." Wes smiles, the dimple on his cheek flashing. "And you can call me Ding. I kinda like it."

"Oh, goodness!" Mrs. Mitchell says after a few minutes. "The residents are waiting for a skit! I forgot!"

The five of them look at each other. Lilith clears her throat and shifts to smooth her dress. "Mrs. Mitchell, would you consider a talent show, instead? Ally—maybe you could show them how you juggle that ball? And Jason, you could sketch someone?"

Wes blinks at Lilith. "You don't want to sing?"

She shakes her head, staring down at her bare feet for a second. "I don't really feel up to it. But I have my makeup in my bag. Do you think Agnes would like a makeover or something? You know, she could use a little excitement."

Mrs. Mitchell smiles at them all. "It's been a long day. Why don't we all just go and say our good-byes instead?"

Something rumbles through Rex. Regret, maybe. Why has she introduced them to August? What will they say about him—about her—on Monday? Why did she trust them when they all know they'll only be together this one day?

"Okay," Ally says. "Until next week, anyway."

"Excuse me?" Mrs. Mitchell squeaks, her eyes wide.

"Oh, yeah!" Wes says. "We have to do a prom thing next Saturday! For Judith!"

"What?"

"And maybe we can have our meetings here, you know, for the club?" Jason says.

"The club?" Mrs. Mitchell's voice is high but not sweet. It sounds more like she's panicking.

"Yeah," Jason says and smiles at the others. "The Reckless Club. I'm the president."

"We could meet here, in August's room." Rex's voice goes small again.

"Thursday nights?" Ally says. "Practice lets out pretty early on Thursdays."

"Sure." Lilith nods.

Rex rubs at the sudden heat around her eyes.

Mr. Hardy laughs. "I guess you win, Trish. You were right. They never want to leave."

Rex smiles, then leans forward and tucks the blanket around August so it's snug along his sides. "So, I'm going to go, August, but first, I have some news." She glances toward the doorway where Mr. Hardy and Mrs. Mitchell still watch them. "You know how I was worried about where I'm going to live? I think I have a solution."

Wes shifts. "You do?"

Rex nods but doesn't look away from her brother. "Mr. Hardy says he and his wife—remember, August, you met her last week when they visited?—well, they applied for something called kin-ship care. It means they can be my foster . . ." She gulps. "They can take care of me, if Grandma goes back to Florida."

Wes whispers, "That's awesome." Ally covers her smile with her hands as Lilith turns up the music with a whoop. Jason grins across the room at Rex. Only August doesn't seem to react, his face staying slack. But then his hand contracts, shifting toward Rex. She leans forward, resting her cheek against his palm.

"Oh, Jeff," Mrs. Mitchell says in the doorway and wraps her

arms around her brother. "You're a good man."

Mr. Hardy shrugs. "It doesn't mean, Rex, that you don't still owe me detention."

Even August's smile stretches as the room fills with laughter.

Rex's voice shakes. "I think I'm going to be okay, August."

Dear Northbrook High School teachers and administrators:

You want us to apologize.

Fine, we're sorry.

Sorry that you think so little of us. Sorry that you think
you have all the answers. Sorry that you think this—giving
up the freedom of the last perfect summer day before we
shoulder the burden of your expectations and the bruising of
our dreams to walk the halls of Northbrook High School as
freshman—is a worthy punishment for our crimes. Sorry that
you think being here was a punishment at all.

You want us to tell you what we've learned today. But maybe
you're the ones who need a lesson.

You see a Nobody, a Drama Queen, a Flirt, an Athlete, and a
Rebel when you look at us. But after today, we just see each
other. And we're going to change things, make them better,
starting now.

Sincerely,
The Reckless Club

AUTHOR'S NOTE

If you (or someone you know) is feeling self-destructive, help is available. You are not alone. You are loved. You are needed. You are precious. Please call the National Suicide Prevention Lifeline at 1-800-273-8255.

If you're being bullied or witness someone else being affected by it, please talk with an adult you trust. If that adult doesn't listen, find someone else. Keep talking, be loud, and get help.

ACKNOWLEDGMENTS

This past year has been a whirlwind, filled with new books, new friends, new experiences, and new challenges I never could've anticipated and never would've enjoyed without the support and comfort of family and friends. Thank you.

Much love and gratitude to superagent and incredible human Nicole Resciniti for being a pillar of strength, encouragement, and wisdom. I love you, Nic!

Thank you also my phenomenal editor Julie Matysik. What a tremendous joy it is to work with and know you! I'm grateful for your expertise, coaching, and friendship (and sweet baby pictures).

Many thanks to the entire Running Press team, including publisher Kristin Kiser, marketing director Jessica Schmidt, children's publicist and marketing manager Valerie Howlett, marketing manager Geri DiTella, creative director Frances Soo Ping Chow, copy editor Susan Hom, and project manager Julia Campbell. It's an honor and privilege to be part of the RPK team.

Much gratitude also for Nia Kingsley for her tremendously valuable insight, adding to my understanding of what Lilith would experience as an Indian American and an actress. Thank you also to Shikha Patrick, who also shared her perspective. I'm so grateful.

I'm also grateful to my critique partners. Thank you Susan Haller Jennings, Lynn Rush, and Emma Vrabel for your spot-on feedback, especially when it's not what I want to hear. I'm blessed to have such talented friends.

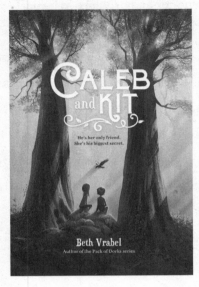